# The
# Court
## of
# Vintage
# Woods

## JOSH PENZONE

an imprint of Sunbury Press, Inc.
Mechanicsburg, PA USA

an imprint of Sunbury Press, Inc.
Mechanicsburg, PA USA

For information about special discounts for bulk purchases, please contact Sunbury Press Orders Dept. at (855) 338-8359 or orders@sunburypress.com.

To request one of our authors for speaking engagements or book signings, please contact Sunbury Press Publicity Dept. at publicity@sunburypress.com.

ISBN: 978-1-62006-166-4 (Trade Paperback)

Library of Congress Control Number:  2019948993

FIRST BROWN POSEY PRESS EDITION:  September 2019

*Product of the United States of America*
0  1  1  2  3  5  8  13  21  34  55

Set in Bookman Old Style
Designed by Crystal Devine
Cover by Lawrence Knorr
Swirl art from http://clipartmag.com
Edited by Lawrence Knorr

*Continue the Enlightenment!*

For Laura

# Contents

@

# Previous Publications

THESE STORIES have appeared in (slightly or very) different form in the following publications: "The Whitings" by ELJ Publications as a stand alone title, "A Soldiers Story" and "A Return" in *Blue Lake Review*, "Falling Away" in *Five on the Fifth*, "Rose" in *The Critical Pass Review*, "The Scratch" in *Chantwood Magazine*, "After Zion" in *FICTION Silicon Valley*, and "Escort" in *Sediments Literary-Arts Journal* (under the pseudonym Michael Shire).

# Acknowledgments

THIS BOOK ORIGINATED as my master's thesis at Wilkes University, but it wouldn't have survived beyond that purpose without the wisdom and encouragement of Sara Pritchard. Sara, your belief in these stories transformed me as a writer. Thank you.

Since this is my first book, I have a lot of people to thank. Thank you to the early readers and your comments: Regina Meyer, Sylvia Bower, Kaylie Jones, Kinsey Cantrell, my Wilkes cohort, and Nick Penzone. Kurt Dinan, thank you for your publishing advice. It led me to where I needed to be. Gail Galloway Adams, I've never met you, yet you spent so much time giving me wonderful constructive criticism on a manuscript you rejected. Gail, your comments and generosity led me to this final draft. Mom, thank you for buying me my first word processor so I could write my stories as a kid. Pete, thanks for being weird and for helping me understand character development, because yes, brother, you are a character. And a big, gracious thank you to Lawrence Knorr for believing in this collection.

Lastly, to my wife, Laura, this book only exists because of you. You are remarkable. Eliza and I are so unbelievably lucky.

# The Whitings

A T SOME POINT, Ginny Scuro had swapped her digital Casio for the sun's location to tell time. Since then she'd been early often, late frequently, and rarely on time, but today she didn't need that Casio, or the sun, just her motherly instincts. She tried not to worry about Liam, but since Adam—her oldest son—had been stationed in Afghanistan three years ago, she jumped to awful conclusions with newfound deft ability.

She'd been waiting barefoot for Liam at the end of her driveway. In case the neighbors were watching—and over the years she'd given them reason to—Ginny Scuro checked her mailbox—yet again—to mimic a sense of purpose. Her breathing quickened as she tried to suppress the image of a bloody Liam crawling out the busted window of a wrecked car. The worst part of this conjuring: as the fire met the glistening streak of gas, spitting back a blazed line towards his soon-to-be-charred-body, Liam chose to call out to his father—instead of her—for help.

"Figures."

She toed a weed sticking up from a crack at the end of the driveway with her shoeless left foot, wondering if it made the weed less lonely.

"Ginny," Karen Whiting said, crossing the street, brandishing mail. "Guess who's got your *Entertainment Weekly*. Again." Karen handed her the magazine. Ginny didn't look at it. Karen's smile distracted her.

"Thank you," Ginny said, rolling up the magazine and pointing it at the Whitings' home, using it as a scope.

Karen pointed at Ginny's bare feet.

"Trying to catch pneumonia? It's dropped like twenty degrees since this afternoon."

Ginny rotated the makeshift spyglass away from the Whitings' bedroom window to Karen and then laughed.

Years ago, a therapist said laughing would acknowledge her own oddities, helping the opposing person feel less alienated from her—as the therapist put it—*originality*. That therapist gave great advice, but she stopped seeing him because she didn't like his gilded-rimmed glasses and kind face. How could a man who looked so benign be keen enough to dig up truths she had interred and hidden from herself?

"Pass," she said, which confused Karen. Ginny smiled like she was posing for a sorority composite, hoping Karen would notice she'd been whitening her teeth.

"You should be wearing shoes," Karen said. "And a coat."

Ginny's condition wasn't a secret. When she went off her meds, she did unusual things: spray painted a neighbor's lawn pink, stole all the Christmas lights on the street and rolled them into a huge ball, dug a hole in the back yard filling it with water calling it a spa . . . but it was always harmless. The night Liam left for college, the house felt still, as if it no longer had a pulse. Sadness attacked her. She never realized the house was alive. After she stopped crying, she began scrapbooking about her "Crazipades"—as she called them—but when her husband discovered the book, he threw it out. "It's not healthy to put a spotlight on your illness." Since then she'd become socially dormant and now she wondered if she'd spent the last two months waiting at the end of the driveway for Liam to come home.

"I'm waiting for Liam," Ginny said, scratching a pretend itch. "He's coming home from Miami University for a few days. Fall break."

"Miami! How did I not know that he went there?" Karen said. "That's where Bruce and I went! Oh, how we loved it. Nothing like falling in love at Miami. Do you know what they call couples that get married after meeting there as students?" As Ginny shook her head she imagined a young Karen and a young Bruce Whiting kissing in the rain, as couples do in movies. "Miami Mergers. Isn't that fun?"

Karen smiled. She had perfect white teeth. No prominent canines. Or prominent front teeth. Just perfectly symmetrical teeth behind her perfectly full lips. Karen Whiting was the reason she'd begun whitening her teeth. She put the rolled-up *Entertainment Weekly* to her right eye and spied the Whitings' upper left window. Her imagination moved Karen and Bruce Whiting from kissing in the rain to making love in their bedroom, where they simultaneously climaxed. Perfectly.

She moved her scope around the neighborhood. Two houses down at the mouth of Vintage Woods Court, Howard Havenshaw saluted Ginny. He then lowered the American flag, its fabric undulating in the gleam of the October twilight. Ginny unrolled the magazine.

"I don't like this game anymore." She gave the magazine to Karen, who twisted it, wrinkling the cover.

"He shouldn't even look at you." Karen's soft hand warmed Ginny's arm, combating her goosebumps. Karen seemed to know about Howard Havenshaw too. Ginny didn't care how or why. It was nice she was on her side and nice she didn't have to explain.

"It is what it is." Ginny sighed. "We are what we are," Ginny said, mimicking a line she'd heard on a trashy mid-day talk show. With both her boys out of the home and her husband always at the restaurant, Ginny had spent her days identifying with the irrational people on sensationalized talk shows. At the end of an episode of *Maury Povich,* a young mother had issued nineteen paternity tests to nineteen possible fathers. When none were proven to be the father, Ginny sobbed, until her entire body ached.

"You're stronger than I am," Karen said, glaring, as Howard Havenshaw folded the American flag and walked it to the pole. "I'd tell him every day what I thought."

"Who's to say Adam wouldn't have enlisted if there was no such thing as Howard Havenshaw?"

"Still," Karen said, rubbing her flat stomach, pivoting to look at her home, "I can't imagine having a son on the other side of

3

the world at war. I *worry* when Bruce is on a business trip in Minneapolis, staying at a five-star hotel."

"Like all unwanted things, you get used to it." This was another talk show platitude, or from a bumper sticker.

A car pulled into Ginny's driveway. A tall, good-looking young man stepped out. He slammed the door and took two long strides to the trunk, pulled up a laundry basket of dirty clothes and pointed at Howard Havenshaw. "That dick saluted me. Seriously. What a dick." He looked around. "I thought Dad would be home. Whatever. What's for dinner?" Before Ginny could tell him *nothing*, he said, "Doesn't matter. I'm working at the mall this weekend for extra cash. I'll pick something up at the food court." He made a smooching sound as he passed.

She offered Karen one of those dumb smiles used to replace dialogue. She'd often seen this expression given by guests on *Dr. Phil* after Dr. Phil had forced them to discover an unwanted epiphany. *You see now how you hurt others, don't you? You see how now knowing this about yourself, you are now willing to change, to now accept responsibility, to be a better person now?* The guests would nod while crying. Maybe the tears were tears of joy for feeling compunction when realizing they weren't sociopaths. Perhaps that was the true epiphany.

"He sure is a good-looking boy, Ginny. I bet he has to beat them off with a stick."

She thought back to Liam's eighth-grade year when he first realized his good looks made life easier. Sometimes she didn't know whether to be proud of her beautiful creation or embarrassed by his smug actions.

"We should get dinner this weekend," Karen said. "Bruce isn't coming home. Something about a hostile t—" Karen looked back at her house, giving it the same dumb smile Ginny just gave her. "Shit," she said, checking her pockets. "I shut the door in the garage. It locks automatically, like a hotel door. I'm such an idiot sometimes."

Karen grabbed Ginny's hand and guided her across the street towards the beautiful brick home. Excitement overshadowed Ginny's pain from walking on bits of gravel. Karen pointed at the mulch bed along the left side of the house and directed Ginny to look for a fake rock. Ginny picked one up and shook it. A key danced inside.

"Thank you," Karen said. "I can never find this thing and I lock myself out at least once a month. It's like I don't even want to be in my own home." Her words were flat, like a joke that missed. Karen led Ginny to the front door. She opened it. To Ginny, the inside of the Whitings' house looked like one of those stores in the mall that mocked her for not decorating a welcoming home.

"Here," Karen said, handing her a key. "I want you to keep this so when I need it, you can rescue me." She placed the key in Ginny's hand and curled her fingers around it as if the key was a precious family heirloom, and this was the ceremony to entrust Ginny with it.

@

Her husband's snoring sent her to the basement. Ginny labeled boxes and packed the space across from the water heater, floor to ceiling, leaving the large room empty.

"Finished."

She admired the way she'd stacked the organized contents of each box according to the person it belonged to. One day Liam would want to go through his past, same with Adam. Yes, they'd appreciate this, one day. Plus, when she got around to it and asked George to leave, this would expedite the matter.

As she sucked the cobwebs out of the support beams with the Dyson, she remembered how George had promised to make a game room for the boys when they were little. Maybe she would do something with the space since George never did. She contemplated making the space look like a showroom from Restoration Hardware, but before she could make plans for it, footsteps shuffled above, cuing her routine.

Her adrenaline pulsed, creating too much energy to scramble eggs or to brew coffee or to ask about last night's restaurant's business. She sang a sonnet. The opposing wall craved to be a prolific painting of the Italian countryside. In high school, she was one of five chosen to paint the senior mural on the cafeteria wall. She couldn't remember what they painted, but she remembered laughing and how the tension in her shoulders vanished being around like-minded people.

"Maybe I should join Facebook."

"And then move to Florida, and eat dinner at three in the afternoon, and watch your skin lose its battle to gravity, like all other old people," Liam said, entering. Without making eye contact with Ginny he opened the refrigerator and said he was working a double shift and wouldn't be home until late. He worked as a model that stood—sometimes shirtless—at the store's entrance to lure teenage girls inside to shop. George said he had two big Friday parties and he'd be home late because they were understaffed. He looked at Liam.

"It'd be nice if one of my sons was interested in the business their grandfather started over fifty years ago."

"I'm not changing my major, so hire a managing partner already."

Ginny picked a clean glass from the cabinet and scrubbed it.

"Liam, I don't expect you to understand this, but hiring a manager I can trust is a little more complicated than—"

"Whatever, Dad. Good people are out there. Find one and allow 'em to close your beloved *restaurant*. Stop working fifteen-hour days. Maybe even escape that heart attack that has you in its sights."

As Ginny ran another clean glass under sink water, she hummed a song from high school. She couldn't remember the title, but she remembered dancing to it at a party. Colored bulbs replaced all lights. It was like being trapped inside a Crayola box. Drenched in sweat, she danced, lost in that vibrant kaleidoscope. Alive.

Liam blew her a kiss and promised to catch her up on all things Liam *later*. George kissed her cheek and said she shouldn't wait up for him. Ginny laughed. George cupped his hand under her chin and stared at her as a physician might. He petted her bicep and reminded her to take her pills. She lied and said she already had.

@

The October breeze tickled her cheeks as she strolled between the symmetric rose bushes of the Whitings' walk. The key slid into the lock. She looked back at her home. The light blue paint appeared off-white. Turning away, she pushed the door open.

The tile floor in the foyer looked Italian or Spanish, but having never made it out of the country, Ginny could only guess. She sniffed the blue silk flowers set on an oak table, their stems wedged between clear marbles. The granite-looking countertop in the kitchen felt more like recycled glass. She poured wine from one of the three opened chardonnays she'd found inside the stainless-steel refrigerator into a coffee mug with a palm tree embossed on it and strolled through the living room like she was at an open house. Her finger found no dust as she ran it across the top of a mahogany bookcase. She smelled the daisies in a water-filled pink vase, but like the flowers in the foyer, they too were artificial, although they could have fooled a florist.

She curled a red scarf she'd found draped over a chair in the kitchen around her neck and stroked its silk fabric. In the master bedroom, she sprayed a perfume called Narcotic Venus on her neck and wrists and clothes. The scent summoned scenes of Karen at the Labor Day cul-de-sac barbecue last month, turning heads in her green sundress.

Dresses that still had tags lined the master closet in a color-coordinated design, making the middle wall look like a rainbow. On a shelf underneath that green summer dress that had stolen glances from everyone at the party was Bruce and Karen's wedding album. The Whitings married on a beach twelve years ago. Bruce had aged better than Karen, but Karen's natural beauty still commanded attention. Ginny herself wasn't unattractive, but the pills always made her feel sluggish and frumpy like everything was happening too far away from her to care.

Except for a telescope, the bedroom at the end of the hall was empty. She wanted to look through it but became distracted by the blades of grass sprouting from the white baseboard. Closer, she realized they weren't blades of grass, but flower stems, like the ones in nursery displays at Pottery Barn Kids. She peeled off a stem and then tried to re-stick it, but it wilted.

Back in the empty room in her basement, Ginny stuck the stem on the plastered sheetrock. From her pocket, she pulled a picture she'd taken from the Whitings' wedding album. A crease had formed down the middle, separating Karen Whiting from her bouquet of reds and violets and yellows. In it, Karen looked over a balcony, out to the beach, away from the camera. The sun shone in the background—Ginny guessed it to be about six o'clock beach time. The white dress cinched Karen's waist and hugged her breasts. Her neck was long and sensuous and her full lips pouted towards the blue sky. She looked so strong. So confident. Ginny rubbed a hand over the photo and cried as she thought about the impossibility of starting life over. To not be sick. To not raise one boy who chose war over family. To not marry a man who loved work more than her. To not run out of things to say to her young-est son. To touch the impossible. To harmonize an individual exis-tence with motherhood. She squeezed the Whitings' key, its jagged teeth imprinting on her palm, wishing its mark indelible.

@

The next day she entered the Whitings' bed. She didn't mean to, but it looked so enticing, made-up as if prepared by the Waldorf. Once under the covers, she couldn't seem to get close enough to the sheets. What were they? Fifteen-hundred thread count? She removed her sweater, then her slacks. Still not close enough. She pulled down each sock with the opposite toe. Still not close enough. She unhooked her bra and removed her underwear. She moved until she grew warm. Then, as if she had no choice, she placed her hand between her legs and imagined staying there until the Whitings returned. They would smile with relief, glad that Ginny had read their signs at social functions, pleased they didn't need to broach the taboo subject of a three-way. They would strip down and get into bed on either side of Ginny, warming her with their bodies. She'd come without giving instruction. Perfectly.

After the heat had left her shoulders, she admired a large framed photograph above the headboard. It couldn't have been just a yellow splotch. There had to be more to it. These were the Whitings. It must be art. Maybe it was a lily engorged with life, or maybe it was an accurate depiction of the sun. Naked, she stood on the bed and walked towards the picture. The closer she got, the blurrier it became. Perhaps she needed distance. She stepped off the bed and walked backward across the room, but was distracted by the cracked bedside table drawer. Inside were books on fertility and a calendar to chart ovulation. The day circled for maximum chance of conception was today. Bruce was still out of town. Karen had left for a day trip to visit her mother, or so Ginny had read on the refrigerator calendar the day before. She flipped the pages backward. Five months ago a happy face grinned with a note that said, "And baby makes three." In the telescope room, she pointed the lens at the sky, the same sky that could see Adam in Afghanistan. She thought about asking it if Adam was okay, but didn't, afraid she'd hear an answer.

Using matching sheets from the linen closet, she made the bed and then stuffed the dirty Hotel Grand sheets into a pillowcase to take home. They smelled like musk and Narcotic Venus and her. She wondered if Liam changed his sheets in college. A year ago, he acted like a lunatic and yelled at her to leave his room, demanding that she respect his privacy. She didn't like seeing him irrational. Worried he'd end up like her, she never went in there again, not even to clean. A few times before he left to study engineering at Miami University, she sat outside his door and took dictation: names of friends, titles of songs, video games he played, dialogue from the porn he watched. Most of his Facetime sessions dealt with schoolwork. Liam seemed to be the smartest amongst his friends. She'd draw hearts as he explained the meaning of *The Awakening* to kids in his AP Literature class. She never worried about him catching her scribbling on her notepad because he had his own bathroom, and last Christmas she'd bought him a small refrigerator (against her husband's wishes) so he wouldn't catch her spying. The hug he gave her when he opened it was worth the onset estrangement.

Still naked, she ran her hand across the clothes in Karen's closet. Why didn't Karen wear these dresses? When she got to the green one, she slipped it on. She was the same size as Karen, but with smaller breasts. Nothing a good bra wouldn't fix. She put the clothes she'd worn to the Whitings' in the pillowcase with the sheets and wore the green dress home.

George's car was in the driveway. She stuffed the pillowcase holding the sheets and her clothes behind a beige bin full of gardening tools in the garage.

She entered to a smiling George sitting across from Florentine fish. Her favorite. She sat at the table.

"It's cold now," he said, pointing to the dish. "Where'd you get that dress?" When she didn't answer he cast a scrupulous glare—her every movement seemed to be something worth analyzing—so she stopped moving.

He heated the fish in the microwave.

"Made the potatoes today. Even whisked cheddar in them for you." He folded his arms as the microwave hummed. "Where did you get that dress?"

"Banana Republic. I liked it so much I wore it home."

George tilted his head to look under the table at her bare feet, and then at her car keys resting on the counter.

"Really?"

"I wanted to feel the grass on my feet one more time before winter strangled away its warmth."

"Very poetic."

The microwave beeped.

He served her the fish but didn't sit, hovering. Its deliciousness made her feel gigantic and clumsy. She stopped eating.

"I talked to someone I knew from years ago. Good guy. Went to Aquinas with him. He's done being retired. He's bored. Ran the Iaconos off Cemetery for years." He paused. "I would be home more. Who knows? We could even travel."

When George had a purpose he'd build up to it with clues. It was his way of getting her to follow an order. She dropped a napkin on her plate.

"Just tell me already, George."

Exhaustion seized her eyelids, which she didn't understand. Her mania should push her forward, but with George, she still felt like she was on her pills.

"Ginny."

He sat down.

She stood up.

"Just tell me, George."

He stared at the half-eaten fished blanketed by the napkin.

"I had an affair. I met her at the food show in Toledo last month."

"Is she prettier than me?" Ginny read the numbers on the microwave, quadruple zero.

"No."

"Younger?"

"Yes."

"Why?"

"I don't know." He shrugged. "We laughed. I guess," he paused, "it felt good to laugh."

She took a bite of fish. She knew George had breaded it himself and pan-fried it in oils and cut the fresh spinach and baked it in homemade red sauce and topped it with shaved Parmesan and garlic.

"No. Not why you did it." She took another bit. "Why tell me?"

George set her pill container next to the plate.

"Adam is coming home at Thanksgiving. You need to be right to see him."

She looked at the Tic-Tacs she'd placed in the container.

"Adam's coming home?"

"Please don't read into this. I didn't know either. Liam told me. He was planning on surprising both of us. Listen," he said, grabbing her hands, "you need to be right when he comes home."

"Be 'right?'"

"Adam could still reenlist. Keep his active duty. We can't risk not being a family again. No more secrets. No more lies." He gave her a hard look. "No more affairs. No more distance. This is *our* chance to start over."

When he opened the cabinet and grabbed the pill bottle she felt like she'd been pushed out a moving van. He grabbed her wrist and waited until her hand opened. He nodded towards the glass of water on the table. The bags under his eyes were new. His crow's feet crease had deepened. She thought he'd aged well, but maybe she'd been wrong. When did his top lip get so thin?

"Ginny. Please. Think of Liam and Adam. Please."

She put the pill in her mouth.

He told her everything would be okay. He told her she didn't have to tell him the true story about the dress as long as there would be no fallout from it. He told her he loved her and that he would be home more and that they would take a vacation or sign up for dance classes or an art class or just get in the car and drive. Anything. Everything. He told her all the promises she'd assumed when she'd married him. And as he did so, she kept staring at those zeros.

@

The next morning Liam slurped the multicolored milk from the bottom of his cereal bowl. George sipped his coffee. Ginny made sure George watched while she put the pill in her mouth. Afterward, she cleared the plates and moved to the sink. She rubbed her tongue over her teeth. The aftertaste of what her latest doctor called "mood stabilizers" pinched her taste buds. She washed the same plate over and over until Liam and George left. With the house echoing silence, she put on her tennis shoes and walked outside.

At first, she thought she'd just run to the mouth of the cul-de-sac. Then she thought she'd run to the end of the street, leading her out of the Estate at Tall Pines. Then her legs took her to the main road. From there she made a left onto another main road. Was she going North? West? She didn't know. Her lungs felt heavy. Could be South. Something burned in her shoulder, but she thought about Adam and kept pumping her legs. Soon she was in the country, surrounded by dead cornstalks. Hands on hips, she gasped for breath. The temperature had dropped. Cool sweat moved down her forehead, to her chin. Two miles from her home and it seemed like another world, a simpler world. She sat down in the dusty dirt and looked at the cornfields. When she was little her grandpa would drive by farms and guess a farmer's work by the corn. "Look, Doodle," he'd say, pointing to a field of six-foot-high corn. "That farmer is something-else. Each stalk is calculated with careful precision. Each stalk is straight and tall and the same space apart." Ginny asked if it made the corn taste better. "Taste is taste, Doodle. What you are looking at is pride. Pride in what you do shows you the map to life."

Three gunshots fired seemingly reverberating in every direction around her. Drawn to the boom, Ginny walked toward a broken-down farmhouse. She had seen it driving and assumed at some point it'd be demolished and traded for a strip mall. Standing on the yellow lawn behind the farmhouse was Howard Havenshaw. He was setting up bottle targets on a fence post. When he saw Ginny standing in her gray sweatpants and flannel pajama top, he saluted. She saluted back.

"Mrs. Scuro. What are you doing out here?" He walked away from the bottles.

"I started running," she said. "Here I am."

Howard picked up his rifle.

"You a good shot?"

"No idea."

"I taught your boy. I'm sure I could teach you."

The rifle was heavier than she thought it'd be. In the movies, they wielded guns about as if they were weightless. Howard showed her the safety and said to flick it to shoot. He pushed the gun in tight, tucking the stock under her armpit, then pointed to the sight and told her to aim. "Squeeze the trigger. Don't pull it. You'll jerk the gun. Just squeeze it." She followed the directions. There was a loud pop and instant recoil. She eyed the sky. Howard laughed. She'd hit the target.

Under a weeping willow, Howard cut off parts of an apple with his knife, letting her choose which bites she wanted. He tossed the core and draped his coat around her.

"I don't like you, Howard Havenshaw."

"I know, Mrs. Scuro."

"I don't trust you."

"I know."

"I don't think you are who you say you are."

Howard looked at the weeping willow.

"See how each branch has sporadic leaf exposure? Means the tree is dying." Howard pointed to his inside coat pocket. Ginny found a flask and handed it to him. "Willows need a lot of water to survive. The pond beyond the brush here is bone dry. Poor willow probably drank itself dead." He took a drink. "One thing they teach you in the Army is how to ration. Carry only what you need to survive. Appreciate each bite of food, each sip of water, each measure of a vice." He took another sip. "But never indulge. Learning to survive in the jungle is all about teasing impulse."

He fastened the cap and motioned for her to put it back. She laughed and took a sip and then another and then she laughed again.

"What's so funny?"

"You only speak propaganda. No wonder Adam enlisted."

"The only hero in war is the one you are to yourself to make sure you survive."

She slapped her knee. "Mr. Havenshaw, you know what I think? I think you were a coward in the Vietnam War. I bet you fictionalize the truth to make it worth listening to, to trick yourself into thinking you can escape what you are."

Howard stood and wiped the earth from his backside. He was physically sound for a man in his early seventies. He ran every day at five in the morning. After Adam left for basic training, Ginny used to watch Howard return from his morning run, wondering if her anger would turn into hate. Truth was, aside from the false neighborly courtesies, this was the first time she'd ever spoken to Howard Havenshaw. All those days Adam spent at Howard's home, working on his truck, learning how to hang drywall, how to fix a garbage disposal, she never once made it a point to talk to the man that had reared her boy.

"Adam's coming home for Thanksgiving, but I'm sure you already know that."

"News to me." He shrugged. "Haven't heard from him in a while."

Howard smiled, but his eyes went soft. She handed him the flask.

"I have stubborn boys. It's like they've spent their entire lives proving they don't need protection."

"Dementia took my old man. Vietnam took my twin brother. All living is, is learning to endure it."

He offered the flask. She obliged.

"Howard—can I call you that?" She waited for him to nod. "We joke, the other women on the street, we joke you act as the protector of Vintage Woods Court. You don't really see yourself as that, do you?"

He gave a sly wink. "I only act if the situation is a true threat."

They didn't speak in the car and Howard didn't play the radio. The gun knocked against the backseat seat buckle. It wasn't loaded and the safety was on, but Ginny still had a sense it was about to go boom.

@

Ginny sat on the porch, sipping green tea, watching Liam play basketball with Lance Reynolds. They were both shirtless. Years ago, after his wife wised-up and left Lance, he put up a basketball hoop. This sent Colleen Kellerman—the president of the HOA— into a tizzy as no one else on the street had a basketball hoop and it threw off the symmetry of the *Peephole*—as Colleen referred to the cul-de-sac. Ginny liked Colleen because she was the only one on the street crazier than she was.

Karen Whiting parked at an odd angle in her driveway. Her heels clicked the blacktop as she sauntered to Lance's. Liam passed her the ball. She raised her skirt, bent her knees and released the ball. She missed. Lance Reynolds said, "Good form," and then dipped his head as if he could see under her skirt. He offered her private lessons. Liam laughed and then gave Lance a high five. They both leered as she walked towards Ginny.

"You have such a good-looking boy, Ginny. You must be so proud of him. And a Miami boy. Gonna be something important in this world, that's for sure." Karen Whiting watched Liam as he dribbled to the basket for a lay-up. She clapped. "Go Liam!" She turned. "I can't stand that Lance Reynolds. Just so gross. I don't care for Colleen Kellerman either, but you'd think she'd do better than him when it came to affairs."

Ginny moved her tongue inside her mouth, reminding her how she'd spat out her pill that morning. She thought about the calendar in Karen's drawer. "Do you and Bruce want kids?"

Karen stared at her house. "Bruce travels a lot, but once he gets that promotion in a few months." Her nodding seemed to finish the thought. "Do you have any wine?"

While Ginny washed lettuce and seasoned steaks and whipped potatoes, Karen drank wine. Karen said she had met a friend for "day drinking" and "online shopping." She poured Ginny a glass, but Ginny said she shouldn't have any due to her medication. Karen joked that there was more wine for her. After her second glass, Ginny suggested Karen eat a dinner roll.

"Did you learn how to cook in your husband's restaurant?" Karen tore at the roll.

Ginny laughed a good hearty genuine laugh as if that was the funniest thing she'd ever heard. Karen's eyes widened.

"I know that laugh. Spill it, sister."

"There's nothing to tell. That's why it's so funny. I met George at his family's place when I was a server. He was fresh out of college. He had ambitions to move to Atlanta to start a chain restaurant with a friend, but his dad faked a heart attack and eventually, George ended up taking over the family restaurant. To upset his father in the meantime, he slept with an employee—me—and that's how it all started. I haven't worked there since."

"Never?"

Ginny shook her head. "George wanted to keep business with business and home with home."

"I'd work with Bruce just so I could see him." Karen swirled her wine. "He's in Minneapolis. St. Louis. Omaha. Topeka. Everywhere but in our bed." Karen took another sip of wine. Liam entered. He bit into a roll and then attempted to scoop potatoes with his finger. Ginny slapped his hand and told him he needed to wait until dinner. Liam said all he wanted for dinner was a hug. She kept him back with a spatula and screamed not to get his sweaty body close to her. Liam taunted her by spreading his arms wide. She closed her eyes and Liam got as close as possible to her without touching. He said he'd be down after his shower and that he expected dinner to be "awesome."

"I swear!" Ginny said.

"He's charming."

"He better not get a girl pregnant with that charm. Oh goodness. Karen?"

Tears streamed Karen's face. Ginny handed her a paper towel.

"I'm sorry," Karen said. "It's just, I saw you with Liam and it was just so nice, you know, how much he loves you. Isn't it something? The love of a son? I mean, I assume it is. Such a good-looking boy. You made him. He's half you. Don't you look at him and see yourself and think, 'Wow! Isn't that something?' I know I would. I'd think it every day. Maybe then I'd stop buying things I don't need. Such a happy, smart, good-looking boy. Must be something amazing, the love of a child. I swear. I could watch Liam all day."

Karen gulped her third glass of wine, then wiped her tears and laughed. "Well, I'm a mess. Just a hot mess."

Ginny leaned forward and stroked Karen's blonde hair over her ear.

"I'm leaving George."

The shock stopped the tears. "What? Why? He seems so great. So witty and funny at parties."

"Yes, he's all of those things. And compassionate. And loving. And when he's around, a great father."

"I don't understand. When did you decide this?"

"Just now. Watching you, I realized that I'm never going to cry over George again, and if that's the case, I should leave him." She swiped her hands as if cleaning them. "Easy-Peazy-Lemon-Squeezy."

"Ginny." Karen reached for Ginny's hands. "I'm a mess. Nothing I do should influence anyone."

"It's because you're a mess," Ginny said. "It's because you're a mess," she said again as if the repetition would decode her purpose to Karen and to herself. Karen shook her head, but her eyes moved to the ceiling as Liam's footsteps hovered. Music played. Ginny knew the song. Liam had played it repeatedly during the summer.

Karen smiled a dumb smile like she'd just figured out a riddle. As that goofy grin stay aimed at the ceiling, Ginny remembered the telescope in Karen's empty bedroom, aimed at her house.

"Do you know this song?" Ginny asked.

Liam's dancing shook the house.

"I don't know," Karen said. "It seems familiar."

Ginny was certain if Karen Whiting wasn't sitting in her kitchen, she'd be in that empty bedroom, and a glint from the telescope would shine towards Liam as he danced naked in his room like some drunken primate.

The steaks' juices popped into the broiler.

As Liam danced naked in front of his window . . .

. . . Half an earth away, Adam lay in the dirt, finger on the trigger.

"Squeeze it. Don't pull it," Ginny said.

"What?"

Ginny shook her head. "You need to see something," Ginny pointed to the basement door.

"What? Right now?"

Something sparked in the oven.

"The steaks seem done."

Smoke spit out the cracked oven.

"You never mind that," Ginny said.

Halfway down the basement steps, the smoke alarm sounded.

"The food is burning."

"It happens."

She took Karen's hand and led her to the dark empty room. Karen squeezed her hand. A pull string illuminated the scene. Karen's short breaths stopped when she noticed the wall. She walked to the green dress resting on a nail hammered into the sheetrock. Her wedding photo thumbtacked beside it. On the floor, underneath the dress, laid out like a bed, were the sheets. On the wall, above the makeshift bed, was the flowerless stem. A clear adhesive kept it in place. She grabbed the picture off the wall.

"When did you . . . I don't understand," She ran her fingers over her smiling face. "You've creased it. This is my only copy."

"That's how I found it."

"Yeah! In my closet! And these? These are my sheets! When did you?" Karen yanked up the sheets. "I mean I know you're sick. The whole street knows—after you spray-painted the Burnish's yard pink—but this . . . this is fucking crazy. Do you have any idea? The violation? Ginny? Do you?" She balled the sheets into her arms.

Ginny knelt and rubbed the flowerless stem.

"I do. I really do."

"You . . . you went into that room? *I* don't even go into that room! You had no right! No right!"

Upstairs a chair dragged across the floor. The smoke alarm beeped.

"Mom," Liam yelled. "Mom, you down there? The food is burning. What do you want me to do? I can't get the alarm to stop. Mom?"

Karen moved the sheets to her left arm and held the photo with her right hand. "You had no right!" She tried to peel off the stem, repeating those words, but she couldn't remove it. Ginny stepped backward. Still crouched and choking on tears, Karen gave one last frantic swipe for the stem. "You had no right! No fucking right!"

"Mom?" Liam yelled. "Seriously! There's a lot of smoke up here! I can't hear anything but this stupid alarm! Where are you?"

Karen made a move to the left, but Ginny countered. Karen moved to the right, and Ginny slid her feet. She grinned. She felt as they were dancing. Karen backed up a few feet and screamed as tears lined her cheeks. Realizing the tears was in response to her *original* behavior, Ginny laughed. Karen kicked the drywall and the stem disappeared. She positioned herself, ready to charge.

"Mom? Are you downstairs?"

Ginny stood with her arms out like a cross, blocking the doorjamb. "Mom? Seriously! I can't see anything up here!" Karen dropped the sheets, but balled up the green dress and placed it in the crook of her left arm. She clenched the picture in her right hand at the crease, showing her face. A crash came from upstairs. The alarm stopped. "Mom!" Karen bobbed back and forth. Ginny kept her arms out wide.

# A Soldier's Story

HOWARD HAVENSHAW STOOD at a bedroom window over-looking his cul-de-sac. He wanted to skip the morning run, but the snap-hooks scraping against the naked flagpole reminded him of his duty. Routine—he had read—was the trademark of a disciplined, military man. So, every morning at a quarter to five, regardless of weather, he could be seen in a matching gray sweatsuit stretching on his front lawn. When neighbors inquired about his ritual, he'd salute and say, "Five at five." The residents of Vintage Woods Court believed the phrase was an Army thing. The truth was Howard didn't know the phrase's origin. His dad said it once, so, he'd supposed it was an Air Force thing.

After he checked his e-mail for correspondence from the Scuro boy, he grabbed a folded American Flag from an empty closet in an empty bedroom, save a mirror that had come with the house. An embossed *Army* cast backward in the reflection. He closed his eyes and stood in the center of the room and imagined Vera's face. After the divorce was final, Howard sold his Indiana coal company to the first bidder. He could've gotten more for his life's work, but Vera hated that coal company and had begged him to sell it and move out of the 'Ton, maybe retiring in Weiser, Idaho, where she was from. Vera referred to Washington, Indiana as a place that didn't understand the existence of other zip codes. "I feel suffocated here, Howard." Howard thought he'd die in the 'Ton. He supposed there was still time.

The snap-hooks pinged in the morning darkness as Howard reached for his toes. The phantom pain in his left leg flared. "Damn that flagpole." Howard's curses moved from the flag to Don Longstreth approaching in a blue running suit with yellow reflective stripes along the legs and sleeves and back and chest.

"Howard! Hey! Right on schedule."

Howard Havenshaw didn't move an inch, making the civilian come to him.

Don pointed to the lit porch, where the flag rested on a chair. "Why isn't the flag up? Shirking your morning duties?" He laughed. Howard didn't.

"We wait till morning's first light."

"That's the rule? Huh. I never knew that. Learn something every day."

"I can see you have an agenda, Longstreth, so out with it."

"Right. Military men don't small talk . . . well . . . um . . . well . . . I've, uh, I've been doing some soul searching, you know, because, well, I've finally forced myself to see that my life is spiraling towards perpetuate misery, and I want to, you know, stop that."

Howard pursed his lips.

"Any-who . . . I thought, that I needed to shape-up. To be a better me, you know? Get my life back. Second chances and all that."

*Over-talking reveals weaknesses, Longstreth.*

"So . . . I want to enlist."

"Enlist?"

"In a sense, yeah. I want to enlist in the Howard Havenshaw training program." He smiled. "Whatever it is you do to look like that, I want to do it too. Seriously, you look like you were carved out of a redwood. How old are you?"

"Age is a construct."

"Yes! Yes. That's the stuff I want to learn from you. Think of me as your cadet." He stood upright and brought his right hand to his forehead. Howard held his position for a second. *Never look too eager.*

22

"First thing that needs to go is that lazy salute." Howard kicked Don's feet together and pushed on his lower back. "Stretch the neck. To the sky. That's it." Howard stood in front of him. "Look me in the eye, soldier. Don't blink. Show me trust. Show me respect. Show me attitude that will never beg for forgiveness in letting me down."

Don's entire body shifted. His eyes gained focus.

"You're twenty-five pounds overweight, Longstreth. Twenty in your gut and five in your chin. Looks like a doughy mold is glued to your jaw. Is that what you want to look like for the rest of your life? An amorphous chin atop a beach ball?"

"No, sir!"

Howard nodded as he circled Don Longstreth.

"What's the real reason you want to enlist, soldier?"

"I'm tired of feeling worthless and helpless."

"A quick and terse response is an honest response."

"Thank you, sir."

Don grinned, slipping from role-playing back to reality. Howard moved to his ear.

"Laughter is lazy focus. It will ruin you. Remember the Scuro kid?" Don nodded. His grin left. "He was a budding delinquent before he met me. He scuffed up our sidewalks with his skateboard. He was caught peeping in Karen Whitings' window. He stole clothes from the mall. Was a 'C' student. When I was done with him, he was a chiseled warrior. Now he fights for your freedom from Afghanistan. Do you want me to do the same for you?"

"Sir! Yes, sir!"

Howard swiveled Don. He pointed at Don's home. It was dark. Lonesome.

"The first day you screw up, you go back to that emotional dungeon, you get me? I don't want to hear about your wife leaving you. I don't want to hear about how messed up your kid is. Only the weak live through an exposition of excuses. Army men act. Army men are not weak! I don't train the weak. I leave weakness for the enemy to define. Understand?"

"Sir! Yes, sir."

Howard nodded and moved to the mouth of the cul-de-sac. Don followed. Howard ran in place, waiting for Don to find his rhythm.

"We jog for conditioning and pacing. Not speed. We will run side by side. This will show the denizens of the Estate of Tall Pines that we are a unit. We will only speak to pinpoint suspect happenings."

"'Suspect happenings?'"

"Affirmative."

"Do you really consider yourself the protector of the neighborhood?"

Howard stared at Don. Don's posture became more rigid and exacting and his legs' movement slowly matched Howard's.

"Let's begin."

Howard followed his usual trail. Don ran beside him. After the first mile, Don began to suck wind and slowed and Howard slowed with him, which encouraged Don to keep going. By mile two it was more of a walk with the motion of running, but Howard stayed right with Don as he panted and gasped and spat until he vomited. "Get it out, soldier. Better to expel than to dwell."

Don continued to run. Howard stayed with him. This was the first time Howard and Don had talked since the incident at school. After the Scuro kid enlisted, Don—being a guidance counselor at the high school—asked him to speak to students to promote the military as a career option.

It surprised Howard to see other veterans there. He was last to speak and in listening to the younger soldiers talk about Kuwait and Iraq and Sudan, a hollow pit formed in his gut. Talking to Adam Scuro, a naïve audience of one was a simple task. As he stood at the podium he turned to the soldiers and saluted them.

"You are all so brave. Choosing to enlist. So brave. I was drafted. Terrified at first. Timid. But then something happens after basic when camouflage and a rifle is the outfit." He made eye contact with the students. "Death and blood and guts. Once watched a commie bleed out to calm myself. Smoked me a cigarette and watched his life leave his eyes as his guts left his belly." He paused. "You'll get the itch to kill because there's power in it.

There's power in not being a civilian. There's power in serving your country. Can you imagine? Your mom and dad can no longer tell you what to do. You enlist to protect them and then, by default, by securing their freedoms, you are free. Being an Army man is the ultimate taste of freedom because you grip that rifle and you look at your brethren dressed just like you and know freedom is power. You give that power to citizens of this great country. That gift will make you feel like a God." He then told graphic story after graphic story, as he'd learned, the more intense and detailed the drama, the less likely people were to ask questions.

That evening when Don talked to Howard, Howard was five scotches deep. He shrugged when Don told him he'd had angry parents call about his presentation.

"Couldn't you have held back a little?"

"People want truth, not a show."

"Well, you're barred from the school."

Howard mumbled something as he squeezed a cell phone.

"Is that a flip phone?" Don asked.

Howard nodded and held it up. "Burner phone. CIA shit. I got all the gadgets."

"You drunk, Howard?"

"Affirmative."

Don sat down. Silence connected them.

Sometimes at night, after Howard had stopped thinking about his wife and his brother and his dad and his mind matched the stillness of the dark, the silence allowed him to think as himself. He hated those moments.

"Spy shit, huh?" Don said.

"Affirmative?"

Until he came over in his ridiculous running outfit, that was the last Howard had spoken to Don Longstreth.

"Holy shit. I'm out of shape," Don said, leaning against Howard's mailbox. The sun was finding its place in the sky. Howard motioned him to the flagpole.

"Okay, soldier. We are to unfold the flag and attach it to the pole. The flag cannot touch the ground. The flag is to be raised briskly. You will salute while I raise it. Copy?"

25

They raised the flag.

"Good first day of training, Howard. Thank you for the pain. I'm gonna go and take a long hot shower, so I can cry in private. Man, I hurt. I think the peace treaty I had negotiated with a sedentary lifestyle has officially been broken. My body has engaged in civil war." Don grinned. "Until tomorrow morning then."

"Soldier, you'll see me at precisely nineteen-hundred hours for the twilight's last retreat."

"The what?"

Seeing the Scuro boy twice a day helped build trust. It would do the same for Longstreth.

"The flag only flies in the light. See you at dusk, soldier. Dismissed!"

They saluted.

As Don limped across the street, Howard considered his recruit. His wife ran out on him and his daughter Nikki five months ago. Nikki was already acting out, dying her hair red, then purple, now blue. Her wardrobe consisted only of skin-tight, ripped jeans and tank-tops without a bra. She had piercings in each eyebrow, her nose, and another in her bottom lip. She snuck weed while she walked her dog. Don had a lot of problems, and people with problems rarely saw things through, but Howard would change that. Yes. He would save Don Longstreth, just as he'd saved Adam Scuro.

@

Howard had created his own code for when to call Rich Clemons. Any month divisible by two and he would call on the date of the next prime number in sequence. Today was October twenty-ninth. He dialed the Idaho area code on his burner phone. After a few rings, Rich Clemons answered. "Hello?" Pause. "Hello?" Pause. "It's you, isn't it? I figured out your code. I served thirty-four years in the Navy. Don't think I wasn't expecting you today. Gonna say something this time? Coward?"

Howard pinched the phone closed.

He moved to another empty bedroom. In the middle of the room, a laptop sat on a card table. He opened his email. Nothing new. He clicked on "Drafts." Every day had an unsent letter to Adam Scuro. He opened a new e-mail, addressed it to Adam Scuro, and typed.

Howard checked his watch and huffed. The kitchen table gave a clear view of the liquor cabinet. "A disciplined man doesn't indulge until the duties of the day are done." He turned from the cabinet and faced his back yard. The giant maples had littered the yard. *Adam used to rake my leaves. Maybe a neighbor kid would do it.* He shook his head. Adam's mother had tarnished his reputation, turning everyone against him after Adam enlisted before telling his parents. "I'll do it right now," he said, pointing at the leaves, but he didn't move. His gaze returned to the liquor cabinet, his only decoration.

@

Don stood at the flagpole, facing his house. "You really can see into every house from here, can't you?"

Howard licked the inside of his cheeks, tasting the mouth-wash. He positioned Longstreth under the flag, told him to salute, and pulled the line. Don caught the flag and backed-up. Howard unhooked it and directed Don how to fold it. To Howard's surprise, the corners were straight and smooth.

"Well done, soldier."

Don shrugged and said he was a Boy Scout when he was little. For some reason, Howard said he was an Eagle Scout.

"See you tomorrow at 0500," Howard said.

"Got time for a drink?"

"COs don't cavort with new cadets."

Don nodded and headed home. Howard felt the chill of the night air.

"Cadet Longstreth. Come inside for a scotch. That's an order."

He poured them both a scotch, neat. Don sat at the kitchen table. Howard handed him the drink, then sat across from him.

"Smooth." Don held the glass as if it were a hot chocolate. He looked around. "You're a minimalist. Thoreau would be proud."

"Pictures and knickknacks are for nostalgia. Nostalgia's for the absentminded."

"Kelly was the clean one. Nikki and I are both slobs. My house looks like we are in the middle of either packing or unpacking." He laughed and took a sip. "This is good. What is it?"

"Macallan 18."

"Isn't that expensive stuff?"

Howard said the only things worth money are freedom and good scotch. Don said, "Cheers to that." He laughed to himself as he stared into his cup.

"So, Howard, you still got all that spy gadget stuff?"

Howard grinned. He knew Longstreth had an ulterior motive.

"Like if I wanted to know what my daughter does in her room, is that something you could help with?"

*Talking shows weakness.*

"Never mind. Dumb. I'm being dumb."

He drank.

Howard stared, not blinking.

"She's just in her room all the time, you know. She never sleeps. Never. I mean, my prostate wakes me up twice a night and I can hear her laughing in her room at two in the morning. I hear like weird 'pings' too. Like 'ping, ping, ping.' Then she laughs. It's . . . you know . . . forget it. Forget I said anything. It's dumb. I should just ask her or open her door. It's my house, right? I can open her door. I don't need a bug or a spy camera—do you have that—no, she would never talk to me again. It's dumb. I'm not talking anymore. I'm dumb. Dumb."

When Howard wakes at 4, Nikki Longstreth's bedroom light is always on.

But Howard kept silent.

Don went silent.

They drank the bottle empty.

Howard walked Don to the door.

"If I ever bring that spy shit up again, just hit me. She'd never forgive me, you know. Spying. That's a deal breaker. It's dumb. I'm dumb."

Don stumbled home.

Howard switched to drinking bottom-shelf scotch and soda. He reread some of the letters his twin brother Joel had sent him while in Vietnam. Howard couldn't serve on account of his busted leg, but he never stopped wondering: had he served, would Joel's foot have missed that landmine?

Their father had favored Joel and didn't hide it. Their father was a bomber in World War II, and he talked about what a great privilege it was to light up the German countryside by pulling a lever. When he'd tell those stories, he'd lock eyes with Joel, ignoring Howard. Howard was the second baby, a surprise. This led to complications and his mother died. With all the fictional stories of glory that Howard had spun over the years, the only life he had ever taken was his mother's.

Against Vera's wishes, Howard visited his father often at the nursing home. In his final days, his dementia erased Howard, always calling him Joely. The last time Howard saw his dad alive, he was sitting in a chair by the window. When Howard bent down to ask him how he was doing, he grabbed Howard's arm and said, "Howard, you won't endure. You're weak. I'm a mass murderer. Women. Children. Soldiers. All dead because of me. I endured. I outlived a wife and a son. I outlived my shame. I endured. You killed the only person who would've loved you. Can you endure that?" All Howard could think to say was, "Dad, it's me. Joely."

@

To Howard's surprise, Don Longstreth was stretching at the flagpole. The sun had yet to peak above the horizon in the windless morning, allowing the snap-hooks to rest.

"Thought you might not make it this morning, soldier."

"Today's an important day. I need this today." Don exhaled. "Do you have any kids, Howard?"

Howard shook his head. Vera wasn't able to have kids, which led to a fight because Howard was fine with it. Vera couldn't believe she married a man that didn't want kids. When Howard told her he was trying to be supportive in a difficult circumstance, Vera said she was relieved she couldn't have kids, because if they did, Howard would manipulate them and make them something they didn't want to be. And although they remained married for decades, Howard felt that every fight afterward was about his indifference to her infertility.

Don struggled with the morning run, as did Howard.

"Holy shit! Is that a wolf?"

A coyote trotted from trashcan to trashcan, sniffing. The click of the paws against the pavement grew louder and the scars across its face grew more prominent. Don moved behind Howard, making it stare at both of them.

"Did you bring a gun?" Don said. It snarled. "Oh shit."

The coyote charged. Howard kicked it in the face. It squealed a high pitch cry and backed-up. It regained its senses and snarled. Howard made a violent gesticulation and screamed charging it. The coyote scampered away.

"So, that was terrifying!"

Howard agreed, but said, "Nothing's scary after you've been in the shit."

@

Howard sipped coffee while Longstreth talked to the police.

"I don't know how big. I don't run with measuring tape and a scale on the off chance I can chart suburban wild game?" He turned to Howard. "What? Howard? At least 70 pounds, right?" Don shook his head. "I didn't put a beacon on it. How am I supposed to know where it is now? I just know it was here, in The Estate of Tall Pines. There are a lot of little kids in this neighborhood. At the very least put out some sort of amber alert or something to notify people . . . thank you."

He hung-up Howard's landline and shook his head. "Moron thought I was lying. Said it was just a dog. So pleased to know that the man who wasn't there wants to tell me what we saw."

Don laughed. He laughed so hard Howard smiled.

"Howard, you jacked that thing in the face." Don mimicked Howard, and kicked the air. "Holy shit! I think you saved my life. Rule number one of jogging in the suburbs: always run with a war veteran." Don checked his watch "Shit! I gotta go. See you tonight? Last retreat?"

"Affirmative."

Again, Don reenacted the kick and recited propaganda military slogans out the door.

Long after Don left, Howard was still smiling. Even while raking the leaves in the backyard, he was still smiling.

@

Howard sat on his porch, watching the flag flap in the oncoming twilight. Six years ago, he asked the Home Owner's Association for permission to put that flagpole in his front yard. "I'm aware that the bylaws of our particular cul-de-sac state our street needs to be congruent and such. No fences. No other landmarks creating aesthetic disagreement, but I believe a flagpole at the front of the cul-de-sac will make this the most patriotic street in the Estate, reminding outsiders of our virtue and integrity." Then he slapped his heels together, stretched his spine, and saluted, which was the first time he'd ever made such a gesture in public. Colleen Kellerman and the Homeowner's Association showered him with gratitude, thanking him for his service and dedication to the country.

And so, the lie began.

He patted the small box in his pocket. He'd even wrapped a bow around it. The audio bug was a gesture, that's all. Don wouldn't have to use it. Not at all. Just a gesture.

He looked over his cul-de-sac. Over the years he'd seen suspicious events, but he kept these to himself, just in case he needed to trade secrets one day. His most recent observations: Lance Reynolds was sleeping with Colleen Kellerman. Ginny Scuro broke into the Whitings' home during the day. Bruce Whiting peeped on neighbors with a telescope. Frances Burnish snuck cigarettes, although she said she'd quit years ago. Nikki Longstreth and the Kellerman boy would run to the backwoods at night. He compiled secrets. He patted the small box, pleased he'd have one more.

Don Longstreth pulled into the driveway. Howard walked to the flagpole. Twilight took its cue.

Don gathered groceries from the trunk and walked to his front door. He fumbled for his keys as he balanced the bags. The keys hit the porch. Don cursed. Howard walked over to help. Don dropped the keys again. Howard opened the door. Don saluted and told Howard to come inside for dinner.

"Dinner?"

"Or we could both eat alone." Don's words were loose and inarticulate.

*He's drunk.*

Don's house was a mess.

"It's my anniversary," Don said, unpacking the bags. He held up a package. "I'd never had salmon before I met Kelly. She ordered it on our first date and told me to take a bite. After I did I was like, what have I been missing?" He unwrapped the package and dropped the fish in a bowl. He poured seasoning on it and added a dash of olive oil. He rubbed it all together. "I bought this meal for Nikki, but when I called her, she told me to stop trying to replace mom with her." He exhaled. "So much fun to be her dad."

Don didn't talk during dinner, and after years of training himself to be silent, Howard didn't know how to begin a conversation. Don reached for Howard's empty plate.

"Kelly didn't talk during meals. Just something I've gotten used to."

Howard thought about Vera and how she'd try so hard to learn about his day or his thoughts while they ate. Growing up, he'd learned never to speak at the table for fear his father would ridicule him.

While Don made Manhattans, Howard scanned the Longstreth family photos. Don gave Howard his drink. Howard stopped at a photo where Kelly had her hands on Nikki's shoulders—she must have been twelve or thirteen—they wore matching necklaces with a silver cross. Don pointed at the cross.

"Kelly's parents were super religious. Practically fundamentalists. I think she married me to spite them. And it worked. They didn't come to our wedding. I forgot they existed, to be honest. They both died last year. Dad went first. Then mom. Both heart attacks. Two days apart. They were buried together. Kelly went back for the funeral. She told us to stay here. Nikki never knew them."

Howard gulped half the drink.

Don traced Kelly's face with his fingers. "She was gorgeous. Still is. Thankfully Nikki looks like her mom." He tapped the glass. "Look at me. I'm a nerd. Unattractive. Unremarkable. I think Kelly chose me because she knew I wouldn't say no. And then . . ." He took a drink. "If she wanted out, she knew I wouldn't be able to convince her otherwise. When you can't barter using love in a lost marriage, what can you use?"

"What happened at her parents' funerals?"

Don shrugged. "She rediscovered God . . . I don't know." He wiped his eye. "When that Evangelist came through town, she thought it was a sign or something. Get this: she told Nikki mothers can't leave, even if they are absent, because a mother's love is eternal, like God's. Then she left." He sniffed. "She sends Nikki postcards. Stupid ones with religious crap on it."

"Does she send you anything?"

Don shook his head. "I don't think I was ever part of her life, not really."

"I don't understand religious fanatics," Howard said, wanting to comfort Don. "To believe so blindly in something in hopes to redirect the errors of life to absolution. Phonies. All of them."

Don tapped the photo.

"My daughter's wearing a cross necklace. Just like Kelly's. This picture is five years old and I don't think I've ever noticed that. What would you say about that, Howard?"

Howard shrugged. "Every end has its clues."

Don nodded. "'Every end has its clues.'"

Nikki Longstreth entered. She giggled at the sight of Howard and then saluted. She walked past her father, up the steps. A door slammed, followed by loud music. Howard rubbed his hands over his pants, feeling the gift.

"I don't know what to do with her," Don said, finishing his Manhattan. He pointed to his head. "This week's flavor is blue." He smiled as tears streamed. "Pretty sure she's doing drugs. And she's up all night doing God knows what. Kelly had a way with her, I just don't know anymore." Don aimed his glass at the ceiling. "I miss you, kiddo. I miss you so much."

They sat for some time. The bass of Nikki's music and the ice crackling in their glasses were the only sounds. Don made another Manhattan.

"Before Kelly said 'liquor is the devil's blood,' this was her favorite drink," Don said, examining the fresh Manhattan. "I have one of these every night. After I'm done, I make another and leave it on the table, thinking maybe Kelly will come back; and if she does, she'll be like, 'What was I thinking? I need a drink.' But, every morning it's still there, just as full." He looked at the cocktail. "This is the last night I do this."

Don set the drink on the table. Circle marks were etched all over the surface. Howard thought it had been part of the table's design.

"This cadet is finished, Howard. Finished."

The bass in the music shifted. Don looked up. "I wish I could see through the floor."

"I almost forgot."

Howard presented him with the bug.

"What's this?"

"Surveillance."

"Wow. You weren't kidding." Don smiled but handed it back. "She finds this and she will never talk to me again." He sighed. "I'll trade her not hating me forever for the mystery." Don wiped his face. "I left work early today. Started drinking around one. I thought about that damn coyote. Being that scared was the first time I've felt alive since Kelly left. Made me want a life. Maybe not the old one, but a life you know?"

Don saluted Howard. Howard saluted back.

"Until the morning."

Outside it smelled like fall, but it felt like an early summer night. As Howard crossed the street a coyote howled. He picked up his pace.

There was a package on the steps, a burner phone. This one had a South Dakota area code. He made himself a Manhattan while he waited for the phone to boot. He checked his e-mail. No new messages. He sipped the Manhattan, and when the phone was ready, he dialed.

Vera sounded the same.

"Hello? Are you the person who keeps calling my husband? Hello?" There was a pause. A bed creaked. Footsteps patterned themselves in quick formation across an old hardwood floor. "Hello?" The voice was softer now. Gentle. "Howard? Howard, is this you?" She paused. There was a gasp. He knew this tone. "Is this really how you want to use the time you have left? You were always, obsessing, Howard?" He analyzed her breathing, trying to decipher concern. "Please, Howard. We loved each other once. Remember me then. Remember me from then saying this to you now: do something. Please. Just do something."

In the garage, he smashed the phone with a rubber mallet and dropped it in a metal bin containing other broken phones. He removed a false bottom from the unlocked storage unit and pulled up a rifle with an infrared night scope and loaded it.

Howard stood on his lawn, overlooking his street. "Let's change the scenery," he said, moving across his lawn to the cul-de-sac's mouth. Above him, the twisting flag's snap-hooks knocked against the metal pole.

# A Return

ADAM SCURO AWOKE on his childhood's bedroom floor. Still in his fatigues, he pulled himself up using his crutches—the last thing issued to him by his country—and sat down on a chair across from his bed. He'd been afraid of that bed, afraid its softness would create a peaceful sleep, trapping him in his repeated nightmare. He looked out the window, into the fading darkness, at the house in front of Vintage Woods Court—*There is no light where the devil plays*—and waited for Howard Havenshaw to enter the scene with a folded American Flag tucked under his arm.

Crutches snapped against the pavement, attacking the morning silence. Adam envisioned swinging one and cracking the old man's skull to empty it of his lies. But his anger dissipated as he enclosed on Howard Havenshaw. The old man's sweatshirt hung heavy. Maybe Howard was shrinking the way old people do. Adam was only fifteen when Howard first spoke to him. He'd missed a three-sixty while skateboarding and scuffed his knee, screaming a curse. "Big words from a little boy," Howard said, sitting on his front porch cleaning a rifle. "You wanna learn to be a man, sonny? Be here tomorrow at 0–500. I'll make a hero of you." Howard cocked his rifled and went inside.

Adam waited, but the old man didn't notice him.

"I see you're still at it." Adam pointed at the sweat stains on Howard's ARMY embossed sweatshirt.

The old man nodded but still didn't turn.

"Five at five. Every morning. God bless routine because a day without surprises is a—"

"Good day to be a soldier," Adam said, finishing one of the old man's overused aphorisms. They both smiled. He wondered if it bothered Howard that he'd stopped e-mailing. "Need help?" Adam nodded at the flag. Howard waved him over. Adam grabbed the flag and Howard fastened the grommets to the metal rings.

"What happened to your leg, soldier?"

"Classified," Adam said.

Howard nodded and then pulled the string, raising the flag. The snap-hooks rapped against the flagpole. Adam listened to its unpredictable rhythm as he stared inside Howard's garage. Boxes stacked upon one another—floor to ceiling—filled the left side. The symmetry was commendable. Four rows wide. Seven boxes high. Three boxes deep. Adam lost his desired thoughts as he stared at those boxes.

"See you at sunset for the night's last retreat?"

Adam nodded, which turned into a mirrored salute. He watched Howard walk past those boxes, back into his house before clicking his crutches against the asphalt. His sticks didn't have to strike the pavement of his childhood street. He could have gone anywhere—to Vegas, to Hawaii—after all he hadn't even spent five percent of what he'd made over the last four years as a private in the US Army. But he came home. Not for his family. Not because he felt lost. He came home to confront Howard Havenshaw, the legendary liar of Vintage Woods Court. He came back for a single truth. A confession.

@

Adam's mom was sleeping on the couch. Yesterday at the airport she'd smiled when she saw him, but it looked off, like an unfixable mistake a painter made when constructing a face. He'd heard from his brother Liam that their mom had gone off the rails again and Dad had made sure she was back on her pills. At the airport he caught her sneaking one while they waited at the luggage carousel. He kissed her cheek and said it was good to see her. She stared forward and said "ditto" as they watched the sleek metal slide around and around.

He sat down on the couch at her feet, wincing at the pain in his knee. After the M.D. extracted fluid to reduce the swelling, he told Adam that he didn't do any structural damage, so if he took Aleve and kept ice on it, he'd be back in action in no time. Adam told him he was heading home for Thanksgiving. His active duty done. The M.D. saluted Adam for his service and handed him some Vicodin. He'd been doubling up on the dosage since.

His mom stirred. "You can take that ridiculous costume off. We all know where you've been. Guess that's why you never called." She licked her lips and faced the sofa. The few times he'd called home, small talk transitioned to silence until one of them said they had to get going.

"When's Liam getting home?" he said, wondering why his father hadn't asked him to go to Miami University with him to pick up his brother for Thanksgiving break.

"Poor Liam." She mumbled. "He'll be waiting in his dorm room all day." She opened her eyes. "Waiting. Like a fool."

Their dad was notorious for being late, always choosing his restaurant, The Florentine, his true baby, making everything else second.

Adam waited for her to sit up, to talk to him. When she didn't, he knelt beside her and closed his eyes. He wished she'd stroke his hair, like when he was little and woke up screaming. She'd sing made-up lullabies until fear subsided and the monsters returned to shadows on the ceiling.

@

He spent the day re-reading *1984*—it was the only book he'd ever read from start to finish. He'd tried reading other books, but when another book was in his hands, something felt wrong, almost immoral. On the page, Winston Smith was obsessively imbibing Emmanuel Goldstein's manifesto, controlling his wanted truth through more lies. Commanding officers joked that Adam was the perfect soldier. They'd say he didn't bog down the mind with superfluous ideas, allowing only room for the essentials.

Liam texted: d-lay.

Trained to not question information, he accepted the text's ambiguity as an order.

After studying the bare walls, he pulled back the comforter on his bed and felt flannel bed sheets, his dad's favorite. Growing up he'd only seen his parents fight when his mom was off her pills, but even then, their screaming felt unnatural, more like bad actors doing a table reading. It was worse when they were affectionate. Last night when his father kissed his mother's cheek, there was a premeditated calculation to it that made Adam itch. All his life he seemed to be waiting for an unprompted moment with his family, some emotional pulsation of anger or fear or spite that came from an unwavering love. Even at seventeen when he'd secretly enlisted, their response escaped fearful words or erratic action. Instead, they issued the same contrived looks: his mother's usual far-away-pharmaceutical-laced-stare and his father's tired-forlorn-countenance.

Adam rummaged through his duffel bag. He took two Vicodin and chased it down with a swig of Knob Creek he'd found behind the flour in the kitchen cupboard—his father's hiding place for booze from his mother—and read until Big Brother imprisoned Winston. Not bearing to read what happened in room 101, he took his post at the window and waited until the sky was minutes away from that malleable pink and purple—Howard's cue.

His mom was still asleep on the couch. He waited for her to wake up, for his dad and brother to walk through that door, for something to stop him.

Nothing.

Crutch free now, Adam limped towards the flagpole.

Howard saluted and pointed to the sky.

"Time of year when darkness seems to roll in faster each night," Howard winked. "Winter's challenge is to make us work more swiftly. Not an issue for us trained men."

Howard lowered the flag to Adam's outstretched arms. Six years ago, when Adam had first helped, he tried to tell Howard what he'd learned in American History class about the night's last retreat. Howard said, "Enough of that tricorn hat nonsense. You want a real military education, kid?" Howard lifted his pant leg, showcasing a horrific scar. Adam marveled, instinctively drawn to the violence and glory of war.

Adam rubbed his knee as he looked at the boxes in Howard's garage, the kind that acquired assembling and could be bought in bulk at Lowes.

Mirroring Adam, Howard rubbed his knee. "I don't know about your injury, but mine's telling me some winter nastiness is brewing. No doubt November will trade this Indian summer for snow in a few hours. Ohio weather."

Adam folded the last of the flag, wondering if his knee injury would one day talk to him.

"Your corners are much tighter than when you were a boy," Howard said, taking the flag. He tucked the flag under his arm. "Time for a drink?"

Adam looked back to his house. Although only two houses away, it looked lost in the only dark pocket of the street, as all the other houses had spotlights aimed at trees and illuminated porches.

"One drink."

Howard poured doubles and held out his glass. "To the greatest nation in the world." They drank. Howard patted Adam's arm. "So, tell me about it."

"It?"

"It! The shit! Army man to army man. Tell me, because there ain't no way you can tell anyone who wasn't in it, least of all family."

"Can I tell you?"

Howard paused, then continued.

"And if you marry one day, you sure as hell can't tell her. I mean, she will be compassionate and overdose you with sympathy, but she will look at you differently as if you've broken her trust." Howard looked away. "I know."

"You never talk about your wife, Howard."

"Different life."

"So was war."

"War never leaves you."

Adam took a bigger sip than Howard's.

"Speaking of which . . ." Howard pointed at Adam.

"What's to tell?" Adam said.

"You were stationed outside Kabul? Right?

Adam pushed his empty glass forward.

"Gotta be better than the damn jungle."

"It's just sad, Howard. Just really, really sad." Adam looked away, taking in the austerity of the liquor cabinet. In Kabul, he'd focus on objects when they'd target civilians in hopes they'd turn informer. Adam was never the talker. Instead, he'd stare at some innocuous knickknack in the room, like a porcelain giraffe, and wonder how it got there.

Adam gulped his drink.

"Easy, soldier. This is the good stuff. Aged eighteen years. Three-hundred bucks a bottle."

"Did you change something?" Adam stared at the bare walls. "The furniture or something?"

"Same stuff. Gotta keep it simple. Man only needs the essentials."

*The essentials? A single man in a four-bedroom, 3200 square foot home? That's essential?*

Adam realized he'd never been upstairs.

"Bet everything's skewed after Afghanistan: 250,000 square miles, forty-first largest country in the world. All those mountains. That's a lot of world to cover."

Adam grinned. The old man had found Google.

"Just saw the one spot. Seemed as big or as small as any other place."

Adam stretched out his leg. His knee felt healed.

"So what really happened?" Howard nodded to his knee and leaned forward. "Take some shrapnel diving behind a tank after a suicide bomber introduced himself to town square?"

"What happened to *your* leg, Howard?" Adam said, careful not to slur, as the Vicodin and alcohol mixed him up inside.

"I told you."

"That's the one thing you've never told me, Howard."

Howard rubbed his leg.

41

"What does it matter?"

A text from his brother: DETOUR on 70.

Adam turned off his phone.

"In a Howard Havenshaw tale, everything matters: from drop-lets of water on a leaf, to the sun's position, to the thickness of the bayonet, how much sweat in the boots, and the stench of the fart of the guy in front of you. All of it mattered."

Howard's eyes widened.

Adam's eyes narrowed.

"Adam," Howard shrugged. "Did I do something?"

Adam hit his knee. He hit it again. Nothing. No pain. He jumped out of the chair. "Let's change the scenery."

"Hey! Marvin! My buddy Marvin Kipler from my second tour in Nam said that every morning before we set foot on the trail."

Adam's grin conjured a dumb smile from Howard, looking like he'd forgotten a punch line to a joke. Adam leaned in. "Come on, Howard. Let's change the scenery."

The Barrel 44 bartenders flashed white teeth as Adam and Howard passed. Adam eyed the chalk-written-whiskey-menu on his way to an empty booth in the back. Howard looked around. "You sure about this place, soldier?"

Adam didn't answer. He waved over a server. Howard sat down. When the server told them they didn't carry domestic bottles, only craft beers, Howard said he'd be fine with nothing. Howard looked at Adam. Once a bunkmate had returned from recon and all he had to do was give Adam a look and Adam knew everything from that look. No words needed to be closer for it.

"I think we should leave," Howard said.

"This booth's wood is nice. Not like the shitholes in South Carolina during basic. Tables were plywood or some shit. You should've seen the trash looking for uniforms, wanting to be a stateside anchor, taking the benefits of a guy who couldn't spend his paycheck. I swear. The only way they'd serve this country was on their backs."

Howard checked his watch. An employee opened a storage door and cut into a box and pulled out small boxes marked *cocktail straws*.

"Howard, why are those boxes in your garage."

"What?"

"The boxes. All those boxes? What's in them?"

Howard shrugged. "Nothing." Howard itched the side of his neck.

Adam squeezed his hands into fists. His focus blurred as he felt like he'd been thrown off a plane.

"Oorah!" a blonde at the bar shouted. She slammed down her empty shot glass and flipped the middle finger at three guys.

"Nice ass," Adam mumbled.

Howard raised his eyebrows.

"Howard, my man, it's been so long for me. High school girlfriend gave me a pity screw before I left. I've killed as many people as I've boned. How's that for some Adam Scuro trivia?" Adam opened his eyes wide and laughed.

"You okay, soldier?"

"Hell yeah, I'm okay. No dirt on me! I feel goddamn great! Don't you remember, man! Remember to finally feel free from it? Look!" He pointed at the bar. "They have no idea how safe they are. They don't get it. None of it. Hey. Go over. Tell one of your stories? Like the one you told me about your friend who stepped on the landmine and exploded in front of you. Just poof! Gone! And then his guts rained on you."

"Marvin Kipler."

"Marvin Fuckin' Kipler. Now that's how you change the scenery!"

Adam walked to the blonde. She was about twenty-three and her t-shirt read "Surly Girl Saloon." A heart in the middle of the shirt had a skull with a pirate's patch over the left eye, a bandana covering the scalp. Horns protruded from the skull. The three guys around the blonde wore variations.

"Ma'am," Adam said, "I just heard you shouting on behalf of the United States Marines. Now, those motherfuckers are crazy and great for our country, but they can't touch the Army, ma'am. Not even close."

She looked at his desert camo uniform.

"You on leave, soldier?"

Adam slapped his heals together, stretched his spine, and saluted. "Private Adam J. Scuro. Fort Eggers, infantry in the CFC-A, ma'am. Stationed outside Kabul, Afghanistan. Just ended four years of active duty for the United States Army, ma'am!"

"At ease, soldier." She winked. "My daddy served in the marine corps for over thirty years. Retired now. Even at his age, he said he could still whoop any army man with just his left hand."

"I like those shirts. Got one for me?"

"Why?"

"I'm the only one not wearing one." He targeted both thumbs at his chest. "I look like the enemy."

"No extra shirts," she said. The guys with her shrugged.

Howard moved out of the booth and lingered behind Adam.

Adam reached over the bar and grabbed a piece of chalk then pulled off his khaki tee. He handed the chalk to the girl. "Draw that design on me," he said. "Now, the heart you draw better be the same size as the one you have. The smallest mistake can clue in the enemy."

"You army guys are crazy! I love it!"

The chalk felt rough at first, then its touch seemed to disappear altogether.

"What happened?" she asked, running her fingers on his side.

Adam slid his tee back over his scarred flesh. "It's nothing," he said.

Howard tugged Adam's arm.

"Adam, I think we should leave."

"Private, is this your dad?" the girl asked.

"No," Adam pulled Howard close. "My dad is an un-heroic, small-business owner. This here is the great Howard Havenshaw. The best the Army has ever produced." Adam's tone was flat. "Howard, tell these fine people about the time you saved your platoon when you manhandled the enemy and rolled him on top of the very grenade he had thrown?" Howard tried to leave, but Adam pulled him back. "Or the time you went against your CO's orders because you had a hunch you were being led to an ambush. How your instincts were so keen, you actually ended up ambushing the enemy?" Adam turned to Howard. Their noses almost touched. "Or the time the enemy killed your twin-brother and when he died in your arms how it was like holding your own dead self?"

The bar went silent, waiting for a monologue. Instead, Howard limped to the exit.

Outside, a group of girls' laughter hung heavy as Adam chased Howard.

"What, Adam! What do you want?" The protector of Vintage Woods Court's face was pale and expressionless. He made a violent gesticulation. Adam shrugged and shook his head. He plopped down and scooted back against the façade of the bar. He grabbed his knee. It was painless, but bleeding through his paints.

"Adam, we should get you home."

The tears started when he finally looked at Howard. His body convulsed taking cues from his erratic breaths. Howard stopped pacing and sat next to him.

"My drill sergeant at basic said I came into the Army romanticizing it, like a Hollywood movie or something." He wiped his cheeks. "Said it wasn't that uncommon. Said enlistees do it all the time. Then he asked me my favorite war movie, and you know what? I couldn't name one. Not one goddamn movie." Adam laughed until he found a way to quiet his voice. "I just don't get why you'd do it, Howard?"

"Do what?"

"Make it all up."

The traffic stopped and started and stopped again.

"Jesus, Adam, what do you want me to say?"

Adam closed his eyes. Blood stuck to his pants, and seeped down his leg, into his sock. After his last military post, he'd gotten drunk and found a rock and smashed his knee. He wanted to do it again, but it hurt so much the first time, he couldn't bear it.

With a bum knee, he couldn't re-enlist. And after he did it, fear seized him, because, what if he was right?

Adam looked at Howard. When Howard looked away, Adam shook his head. "Maybe war is peace."

Adam rubbed his bare arms. It'd dropped thirty degrees since the morning. He shivered and thought of the boy, the one who had detonated the bomb, the one who had given him those burns. The boy looked to see if Adam was dead. That's when Adam shot him.

"Pain and regret."

"What?"

Adam stood. "That's what your stories are missing. Pain and regret."

Howard helped Adam stand. When the crosswalk lit white, Howard didn't move; Adam limped past. At some point, Howard caught up, and as they walked together, big wet snowflakes fell.

Howard's garage door opened, but the overhead light didn't come on. The headlights shined on the boxes. Adam squinted, trying to give those boxes a sober gaze. Snowflakes swirled into the headlight's beam.

"Damn garage light is acting up again," Howard said.

Howard turned the key. Everything went dark. Adam opened the door. Cold air swept inside. The hardened bloodstained pants scraped against his knee.

"Wait! Adam. Please wait. Just wait a second. One second. I can make this right."

Howard sounded panicked at first, then his voice steadied.

"Adam, I have something to say. It may not make sense—not at first—but you need to know why I said I what I said. Why I told you those stories. The truth is my twin brother did die over there. I told you his stories. His. Marvin Kipler was real. In a way, all of it was real. I couldn't go. I busted up my leg. The Army said no to me."

Adam looked to his dark house. He checked his phone, one message from Liam: u lost?

"My dad was so disappointed in me. He was an Air Force man. He thought I was nothing because I couldn't serve. I'm just doing what I can here to help the country. This is fine. We are fine. Everything is fine. Just talk to me."

Adam stared into the dark garage. "I just need something real."

"Real? Real? That's what I'm telling you. Adam, listen. Please. Listen. I finally got to pass it on. Don't you see? Together, we are a team. Don't you understand?"

Adam reached over and turned the key. Headlights showed big flakes blowing into the garage. He opened the door empty-ing Howard's words to the night air. Adam's shadow cast over the boxes. He stumbled knocking over a row. "No," he said, tossing aside the jarred lid. Howard's shadow loomed over him, still prattling. "No," Adam said again, as he attacked the boxes inside Howard's looming shadow, opening one after another after another until the last one revealed that they were all truly empty.

# Escort

BRUCE WHITING SAT alone at the bar, rotating his wedding band around his finger. He examined himself in the mirror behind the bourbon bottles. A dimple indented his squared jaw and dark, bushy eyebrows hovered above his blue eyes. Gray, thick hair waved above his ears. He winced, prompting his crow's feet. Botox had become a household joke, and even though he was certain his wife would inject it, he wouldn't for fear people would identify his vanity and talk.

"What can I get you?" the bartender asked. He'd been doing prep work: cutting lemons and limes, spooning out cherries and olives and cocktail onions, not noticing Bruce sitting at Minneapolis's Grand Hotel bar.

"Your most expensive scotch," Bruce said, thinking of his wife in Ohio. *Please come home. Tell work whatever. Just come home. It's that time. What better Christmas gift than a baby?*

The bartender looked over Bruce's three-piece Armani suit. "Celebrating?" Bruce nodded. "One celebratory scotch coming up." He reached up three shelves and grabbed Macallan 25 from the decorative garland and white Christmas lights. He poured it neat and slid it forward. It looked the same as other scotches, and at first, it tasted like Glenlivet, then its smoothness pushed down his throat, warming him, offering no biting aftertaste. The bartender acknowledged Bruce's grin with a thumbs-up. He had assumed expensive scotch was a status thing, a way to show portfolios without exchanging routing numbers, a pricey pretention, but to taste it, was to understand its truth.

48

He finished his Macallan, growing comfortable drinking alone. The barstool was white leather with a hollow space in the middle of its back, just big enough to fit a fist. He tapped his glass. As the bartender turned to grab the bottle, Bruce ran his hand over his right front pants pocket, feeling the newspaper clipping. **Let Chad Fix You** was in bold next to the picture of a shirtless blonde man. A trail of hair under his belly button ventured into his unbuttoned jeans. His chin dipped, doing one of those duck-faces, showing a strong angular jaw, accentuating his cheekbones. His eyes seemed warm, like melted chocolate.

Bruce scanned the room as the bartender poured his drink.

"We fill up around seven," the bartender said.

"I like it like this."

"Me too, but, no action, no money."

After the last negative pregnancy test, his wife cried and told him life wouldn't make sense without a child. He rubbed her shoulders and said they'd keep trying. He wanted to talk about the baby they'd lost, but Karen said never to bring it up. Two Ambiens later, his wife was sleeping and he was calling Chad. A hoarse voice answered. "Who's this?" Bruce said *DJ*. DJ was an office intern, gawky, twenty-two and gay. Once at a Karaoke happy hour, DJ sang "Sex Bomb" by Tom Jones. His playful pelvic thrusts endangered Bruce's practiced reticence. He wanted to jump on the stage, push his backside into DJ's crotch, obliterate all social civility, and let DJ rage behind him until he found an aggressive calm. "So what do you like?" Chad asked. Bruce's mind moved to Lance Reynolds, a neighbor. After a long silence, Chad spoke, as if they were old friends reacquainting.

A group of twentysomethings entered.

"Mind if I close out?"

Macallans were seventy bucks each. Bruce laid nine twenties on the bill and moved to a couch next to a Christmas tree that faced the doorway. The twentysomethings laughed and hollered at the opposite end of the room. He rubbed his back on the couch, trying to appease an itch. On a shelf above him, an androgynous bust with donkey-like ears and horns protruding through the curly sculpted hair stared. If he left now, he could still catch a flight back home. Karen would hug him and light scented candles and put on sexy lingerie. He enjoyed sex with her, but lately, no matter how good she felt, his unbridled desires grew more and more stubborn, and he'd go soft. All he wanted while he was on top of her was for a man to be behind him.

"DJ, yeah?"

Chad was much shorter than he'd imagined—maybe 5'7" in his heeled cowboy boots. Bruce was 6'2" without shoes. Chad's stubble matched the salt and pepper chest hair that popped from under his wrinkled black V-neck short-sleeved-tee. His hair was dark, with bad highlights. He rubbed his chin. Stubble scraped against his hairy knuckles.

"You're DJ, yeah? No one else in a solid red tie." He gave two violent sniffs. Chad took Bruce's silence as an admission. "Chad from the ad at your service. Gonna get some drinks. You imbibe, yeah?"

Chad ordered and then danced in place as he waited at the bar. His jeans were tight and faded with a missing back pocket, but not stylish. His legs looked muscular in his compact form. A brown belt clashed with the black tee but matched his leather cowboy boots. His arms were slender, like wire, no mass, yet toned from his natural musculature. He turned and stretched. Why wasn't he wearing a coat? It was negative three outside. The bartender gave him two pints. As he walked back, Bruce noticed a tube-like indention at his crotch. It had to be a sock or something. It was too cartoony to be real. He put a dark lager in front of Bruce and took a gulp from his glass.

"Started a tab. You'll pay it, yeah?" He sat across from Bruce and grinned as he waved like a magician before the big reveal. "You're a big one," Chad said. He took a sip, eying the ring Bruce rotated. "Let me guess . . . played football . . . star athlete in high school, yeah? Testosterone-fueled existence trapped you into being something you're not, yeah?" He sniffed. Lines creased in his forehead. He had to be at least forty, a few years older than Bruce.

"You try to psychoanalyze all your . . ." Bruce stopped before he said clients. A green exit sign flickered above the donkey-eared bust.

Chad grinned. His teeth were pointed and bleached white. "Just keeping my promise." Chad crossed his leg, showing his boot heel to be three inches. "Part of you is broken, yeah? I will fix that part. Guar-un-teed!" He winked.

Bruce tried not to think about how many times Chad had done this. "So, um, Chad, tell me something about yourself." Bruce looked at his beer but didn't take a sip.

Chad took a gulp, then wiped his face. "Does it matter?"

"Sure."

Chad laughed. "Okay, big boy. Here goes." He clapped, rubbed his hands together, and leaned forward, never losing eye contact. "I'm a college dropout, even though I had an academic scholarship to Central Michigan. Go Chippewas! My dad has a patent on a piece of the artificial heart. My mom taught Sunday Bible study but loved to drink. My brother was killed in Iraq—first war, not the second—I prefer McDonald's coffee to any café in Paris, and my favorite movie is *The Fox and the Hound*."

"Any of that true?"

Chad slapped his thigh then brought his hands together with one loud clap.

"Got me a mom and a pop." He shrugged. "They may have done those things. My brother could be dead in Iraq. Haven't talked to any of them in decades." He made a clicking noise.

"That so?"

"Nope. Just talked to my mom this morning. She's raising money for a special cause: young Democrats that support Trump. But that's not why she called. She called because she needed help with the *New York Times* crossword puzzle. I'm good with words." Chad never took his eyes off Bruce, never blinked. "What is it you do wearing a suit like that? Wait! Wait-a-sec-wait-a-sec-wait-a-sec. Don't tell me. A lawyer. Private sector. I'm guessing . . . probate."

"I'm an efficiency expert. I help companies run more smoothly." Bruce assumed he'd lie about everything, but he needed something to be true.

"So, you fire people. Make them feel shame and doubt, yeah?" He made popping noises with his tongue.

"Not exactly."

"Hey, man. It's all cool to this fool." He finished his beer, then headed to the bar. He did a shot of something and came back with a beer.

"What's her name?" He pointed at Bruce's wedding ring.

"How do you know it's a she?"

"Professional intuition." He drank, keeping eye contact until Bruce spoke.

"Lucille."

Chad brought his beer to his mouth as if it were a microphone. "You picked a fine time to leave me, Lucille. With four hungry children and a crop in the field." Chad stood and belted out a terrible version of Kenny Rogers' song. The bartender looked over and laughed. Bruce rubbed his back against the couch.

"You suck," someone yelled.

"You know I do," Chad yelled back, winking at Bruce. "God damn! I love me some Kenny Rogers. So, how long you been married, DJ?" Chad sat next to him.

The green exit sign flickered.

"I love her. That's all you need to know."

The twentysomethings shared a laugh. Bruce craned his head to look at them. Chad grinned and raised his glass. "To the mysteries of the night." He finished his beer and then chugged Bruce's. He took the empty glasses to the bar and came back with shots. "When did bourbon ever let anyone down?" He took the shot. Bruce followed. His eyes watered as his throat burned.

"You got a room, yeah?" Chad moved his eyebrows up and down as he ran his tongue over the middle of his top lip. Bruce nodded. The exit sign stopped flickering, illuminating green. "Tell me." Chad now bit his lower lip, shimmying his shoulders.

"1424."

"Go there. Order a bottle of wine or champagne or whatever." His mouth moved to Bruce's ear. "I do it all." He turned and rubbed the bust with his hand. "See you around, Pan."

Bruce stood and was eye to eye with the donkey-eared, horned ceramic countenance. The face seemed angular now, sharp in its features, and just before he left, he could've sworn it winked at him.

@

Thirteen floors up, Bruce sat on an aqua loveseat facing a gas fireplace. The coffee table had a gold finish with intricate etchings of flowers along its legs. His suit felt heavy, like a lead vest at the dentist's before x-rays. He stripped to boxer-briefs and stood before an oak-trimmed mirror. Weird patches of hair sprouted all over: back, shoulders, and upper left arm. His bright pink nipples were too large for his chest. His scrawny arms and legs never filled out, teen body limbs on a thirty-eight-year-old. He put on the complimentary white terrycloth robe. It smelled like a hospital. He slipped off his white boxer-briefs and tossed them on top of his suit placed over the leather couch. He grew excited as his skin rubbed the fabric and shimmied the way Chad had when he asked about the room.

Down on the street people walked and panhandled and passed out flyers and fought traffic. Back home, a telescope sat in an empty bedroom designated the nursery. Karen had started decorating it—the ambitious impulse of a prospective mother—but the baby never made it to week five, so the room never made it as a nursery—just storage for his telescope. Sometimes at night, after Karen's sadness and pills forced sleep, Bruce slipped into the nursery and watched the neighbors live their lives. Ginny Scuro cried in silence. Her teenage son danced naked in his room. Her husband was never home. Howard Havenshaw was an alcoholic, yet, even when he spoke to Howard, knowing he was drunk, he still couldn't tell. Must be his military training. Frances Burnish took smoke breaks, but never lit the cigarette. Lance Reynolds masturbated in front of the mirror, never blinking, always smiling. Lance was good looking with a long, straight penis, but that wasn't the allure. He was who he was without apology, and Bruce found that dangerously attractive. He craved Lance's touch, pleasure without reason.

Room service brought a bottle of Shiraz. He opened it and poured two glasses. To ward off nerves, he read *Columbus Dispatch*'s headlines on his phone: a winter storm warning. He was surprised Karen hadn't texted, worried tomorrow's flight would be delayed, making him miss the last viable fertile day.

Maybe she passed out. He'd noticed more and more empty char-
donnay bottles in the recycling bin.

. The knock was playful. Bruce retied the robe with a double
loop and answered. Bubble gum popped as Chad passed. His
arms were red and covered in goosebumps. He dropped a brown
bag on the bed and scanned the room.

"You live good, DJ."

"What's in the bag?"

Chad blew a bubble, then sucked it back, grinning as he
chomped. He clapped. "Time for rules, yeah? Your ass, your call.
My ass, my call. That's it. Ooo. Wine." He picked up the glass,
swirled and sniffed it. "Like the faintest hint of blackberry in
there, yeah?" Chad reached for him, but Bruce circled around the
coffee table.

Chad gulped the wine through his grin and moved behind the
loveseat. He inspected the tag on Bruce's underwear. "Fancy. I'm
a Hanes man." He scratched his stubble.

"Where you from?"

"All over," Chad said, pulling back the satin draperies. He
waved like he was part of a parade. "Usually you guys have a
thing you want. Just tell me that thing." He cupped his mouth.
"Makes things easier. Cancels out all that middle school nervous-
ness, yeah?"

"My thing?"

"Yeah, your thing." He walked over. "Does DJ want a BJ?"

"I've had those?"

"Not from me, sweetheart." Chad winked, as he rubbed his
crotch. "Jeans are tight. Mind if I release the beast?"

Bruce shook his head, wanting to know what prop was used
to create the bulge.

Chad undressed. His unruly chest hair stopped at his waist.
His shaved pubic region revealed it was not a prop. Chad was
huge. Bruce gaped in silence.

"I know, right? Barely tall enough to ride the big rides and
yet I'm equipped with this. You've been with a man before, yeah?
Don't want this thing to deter you."

Bruce's silence made Chad pause. "You have been with a man before." Bruce shook his head. "You like sex with your wife?" Bruce nodded. "So what then? Bisexual?" Bruce shrugged. "Pansexual? Polysexual? Or . . ." Chad slipped his hand inside the robe and rubbed Bruce's chest. "Just curious."

"I just want to enjoy sex again."

Chad rubbed the left nipple.

"You're misplaced is all. Born in the wrong decade. Today, we're all free agents."

"How's that?"

"Judgment is no longer appreciated. Gone the way of the dinosaurs. Let archeologists find the hash-tags in a thousand years." His strong, thick fingers continued to rub Bruce's chest, controlling his breathing. "Welcome to the revolution." Chad kissed Bruce. He tasted of Hubba-Bubba and menthol. His lips were surprisingly soft. "That nice?"

Bruce took a sip of wine. "You hot?" He moved to the thermostat. Chad's arms wrapped around his waist, just like Karen's did in the morning when he made her breakfast. Bruce stepped forward.

"This your thing? Playing hard to get? I like it. It's innocent, yeah? Don't get a lot of you."

Bruce turned. Chad grinned and put his hand on Bruce's cheek. The man in the ad appeared. His brown eyes went soft and gentle and understanding.

"What are *you*?" Bruce asked. "Gay? Bi? Pan-whatever?"

"Whatever's about right."

"You have sex with women then?"

Chad reached for the robe's belt.

"Get as lonely as me, you learn to love everybody. Physical love is the most real love there is." He grinned. "Trust me?"

Bruce nodded, thinking of the time he walked in on Lance Reynolds pissing at a neighborhood party. After he finished, he turned, leaving himself exposed. Bruce stared. After ten seconds, Lance winked then stuffed himself in his jeans and patted Bruce's shoulder as he left the room. Lance was the one he imagined behind him when he was on top of his wife. Lance and Chad had the same eyes.

Chad guided Bruce's hand down his hairy chest, past the smoothness. "You feel that? That's love, DJ." He grabbed Bruce's wrist and moved it back and forth. "For the next hour, we will love each other, yeah? No wife talk. No kid talk. No work talk. No false fantasies. Just me and you. Nothing else. Because if you can eliminate everything and still smile, what's left has to be love, yeah?"

Chad massaged him. They were now synchronized. Bruce turned and put his hands on the windowsill. The window's reflection swelled with understanding.

Bruce wiped the fog from the bathroom mirror. Crow's feet still surrounded his blue eyes. A dimple still sat his chin. His jaw was still square. His eyebrows were still bushy and dark. His hair was still gray above his ears.

The only evidence Chad had been there was the brown bag. He reached inside and grabbed a half roll of Original Hubba Bubba. He popped a piece and chewed. He traded his towel for flannel pajama bottoms and pulled the sheets on the bed back and slid inside. He grabbed his cell phone: no messages. Pings of ice hit the window, making a splintering sound as if the window would crack. With the gum's flavor already fading, he spun his wedding band, then clenched his left fist and closed his eyes. He imagined the promised snowfall and hoped when he returned home, everything would be blanketed in white.

# After Zion

THE CONGREGATION EMITTED a collective gasp as a pall-bearer slipped almost crashing the casket to the frozen ground, but Frances Burnish didn't notice. She'd been admiring her new dress. It was sleek with a plunging neckline. Her son nudged her. "They almost dropped Milton." She nodded, staring at her cleavage. "Your father was a formidable load, David." She glanced at the hole in the ground. "David, did you know your father once suggested—not even in jest—that he ate prodigiously to keep his jaw moving, to burn calories." She grinned. "This morning, before the funeral director closed his oversized coffin, I snuck a pack of Juicy Fruit into his suit pocket. Now he can chomp away to look svelte for the Pearly Gates' red carpet." The pallbearers placed the coffin. As they moved to their seats, Milton's business partner's eyes widened when he noticed Frances' dress.

The preacher raised his palms to the cloudless, gray sky. "Gracious Lord, accept Milton Burnish into your kingdom. Take his hand and lead him through the beautiful pastures of Heavenly Zion, where he may walk with you."

Frances snorted. "Milton hates walks."

"Mom. Shh."

She rubbed the dress's fabric. She'd been the same size all her adult life and still wore clothes she'd worn when David was a kid. "Better to mend than spend" was something Milton would say. She had adhered to his creed simply so she'd never have to hear it again.

"Zion," the preacher continued. "We ascend to see who we were from His perspective."

Frances' thumbs danced across her phone. She hadn't silenced her keypad.

"Mom, what are you doing?"

"Texting your father."

David took her phone. She scanned over the shivering people. Colleen Kellerman waved as if she'd been waiting for her to look her way. Not knowing why, Frances gave her a thumbs-up. Ginny Scuro was crying. Frances wanted to yell, "Wildly wonderful" to make Ginny smile, but she didn't want to be admonished—yet again—by her son, so, she saved their mantra for another time.

A bird flew off a limb knocking snow onto Nikki Longstreth. Nikki gave the bird the bird. Frances laughed. David squeezed her hand, but she didn't lose sight of Nikki. Nikki was a junior in high school. She lived across the street. Frances had caught her smoking pot while walking her dog. Although she'd given up cigarettes to prove to Milton that people could go without vices, she felt nicotine and weed were different. No one ever said marijuana was a gateway drug to nicotine. Yes, she'd buy pot from Nikki, and maybe even dye her hair jet black with pink streaks like Nikki. Perhaps she'd also pierce her nose and her eyebrows and her lip. They'd be twins.

After the service, Frances stared at the open land awaiting more graves. David shivered behind her.

"Your father always wanted to invest in real estate."

"Mom, it's freezing. Can we go?"

She was thankful for the cold. The frozen ground made it easier to walk in her heels.

"We should head back," she said. "Some of my more sociopathic neighbors will be waiting to practice their sympathy skills. You'll like them."

"Mom, I'm going home."

"Utah?"

"Winter semester starts tomorrow. I still need to finalize my syllabus."

She squeezed his arm. "Your father never did have good timing." She looked at the grave. "You could stay. One night? I'm sure the university would understand. I mean, if anyone gets death and religion, it's Utah."

"Mom." David shook his head. "I don't know what to do here. I just . . ." He trailed off and looked at the line of parked cars merging into the fray.

She leaned into him. "Put your arm around me while we stare at your father's last investment. This way, if people see us, we'll look the part."

The winds swirled, but she refused to fasten her coat. Milton complained that she didn't dress sexy, but how was she supposed to when buying new clothes was a waste? David kissed her head, a nice touch for the peanut gallery.

@

Frances stood in her bedroom closet considering changing outfits. She'd bought four dresses for the funeral and was about to take the tags off another—this one backless—when she heard crying. Ginny Scuro sat on her bed, holding a photo of David, a garter snake wrapped around his wrist. He was ten.

"Hiking in Hocking Hills. That was the day David finally got interesting. Happened to be the same day he no longer needed me." She sat on the bed and patted Ginny's leg. "I wonder if I can file a lawsuit against karma."

"The divorce is final," Ginny said.

Frances grabbed Ginny's hand. "Sorry if seeing George today was hard. He and Milton were pals. Milton would have appreciated George lugging him to his final spot." She took the photo from Ginny.

"I didn't see David downstairs," Ginny said.

Frances sighed. "He never had much need for me or Milton. Or people for that matter. We thought about trying to give him a sibling, but we worried David would give him a complex by never playing with him." She tapped the framed glass. "He always liked creatures more than people."

Frances cradled her head to Ginny's shoulder. Ginny's straw-like hair scraped her forehead. Ginny always told Frances that she'd know if she were on her meds because no conditioner could save her hair.

"Is Karen Whiting downstairs?" Frances asked.

"She left the room when she saw me. Poor thing. She's terrified of me."

"You did break into her house, steal a dress, and trap her in your basement while your house was on fire."

"Not all in the same day."

Frances laughed first. Then Ginny. Then the two laughed so hard they missed breaths.

"Karen's sweet," Ginny said, her smile now gone. "Very sad. Sadder than we are, but sweet."

Frances squeezed Ginny tight. "She only seems sadder because she's young. She'll get better at hiding it."

"I miss her sadness."

They held each other.

"You think wherever Milton is, he's happy now?" Ginny asked.

"Milton was always happy. I don't see how the afterlife could change that."

"I hope George is happy without me. Maybe if he's happy, my boys will be happy. If my boys are happy, then maybe even Karen Whiting could be happy. If she's happy, then maybe we can all be happy."

"Wouldn't that be something? A world full of happy people?"

Ginny stood. "I should be going."

Frances grabbed her arm.

"I know it's unfair to say this, but, I miss manic Ginny."

Ginny smiled. "I do too." She hugged Frances. "Sorry about Milton."

Ginny left the door open. Sounds of revelry carried. Frances lay back on her bed and studied the picture of David. "Wildly wonderful," she said, and for the first time since Milton had died, she cried.

When Colleen Kelleman asked how she could help with the "after party festivities" to honor Milton's life, Frances shrugged and said he liked cheese. As Frances moved through the living room, she witnessed Colleen usurping host duties and saying, "Brie? Gouda? Aged Vermont Cheddar?" while balancing a cheese plate.

On the way to the kitchen, Frances received complementary head nods and standard condolences. Frances responded by winking and saying, "Go team."

Nikki Longstreth lingered over the little desserts. She popped an Oreo cheesecake into her mouth.

"Milton loved cheesecake. Mostly for its calories," Frances said.

Nikki laughed.

"Thank you for laughing. People's emotions are so one-sided at these things." Frances studied her pupils, trying to determine if she was high. "Did your dad make you come?"

Nikki shook her head. "Once Mr. Burnish asked how I was doing, and for some weird reason, gave me a gift card to Target." She shrugged. "He seemed nice."

Frances remembered this exchange. It was shortly after Nikki's mom had left her family for a religious cult. Milton despised organized religion, which was the only source of continued contention in their marriage. "Give me a religious funeral anyway," Milton had told her long ago. "Just so you don't have to deal with the holy people." So, when he'd heard that Nikki's mom left her for some traveling evangelistic troupe, he sympathized with the girl and bought her a Target gift card.

The minister moved behind Nikki and poured himself a glass of red wine.

"What did you think of the service?" Frances asked Nikki.

"Guy really liked to talk about Zion."

The minister looked up. Frances waved.

"Religion's like the end to a romantic comedy. It takes you to the shining light, but what then? What happens after glory's promise?"

"Promises are as permanent as the weather." Nikki ate a rasp-berry cheesecake.

Frances walked to the wine station. She smiled at the minister and poured herself a glass of white and took a sip. "I stopped drinking out of solidarity." She tapped her chest. "Milton couldn't indulge. Heart medication. Guess it doesn't matter now. Unless you think your sermon brought him back."

"Frances, the mysteries of mourning are never revealed to the individual. Please come to service this Sunday. I'll want to see how you're doing."

She winked and said, "Go team."

As the minister left, Lance Reynolds entered and poured him-self a bourbon. He lived at the apex of their cul-de-sac. Frances didn't like him, although he'd never personally offended her. At parties, he was always very charming. Yet, she felt like he was someone worth hating, so that's what she did.

"Ladies," Lance said. "Frances, my dear, so sorry for your loss."

"Posh. You're pleased as punch. You'll no longer lose money to Milton on poker night."

Lance grinned. "He was quite the card player."

"I was the only one that could read him. To everyone else he just looked gassy."

Lance laughed. Frances never laughed at her own jokes—Milton always laughed for her—but she almost laughed at that one. Lance grinned as he examined the kitchen.

"Don't get any ideas, Lance Reynolds. This house is paid off and I'm too comfortable and too stubborn to sell. I'll give you the listing after they find my decomposing body binge-watching Netflix."

Nikki spit-laughed cheesecake on Frances' dress.

"I'm so sorry, Mrs. Burnish. That beautiful dress. I'm so sorry."

She wiped the dress with a napkin, but Frances stopped her.

"You worry about it none. Got me plenty of funeral back-up dresses."

"Going all serial black widow on us?" As Lance laughed at his own joke, the recessed lighting glinted off his veneers. Frances grinned at the thought of Lance dying during sex. She imagined him angry, not about his death, but that *death was before climax.* "Came before he came," Frances said, enjoying her own pun. Nikki and Lance shared a confused look. Frances sipped her wine.

"Frances, you still pretend to smoke?" Lance asked. She nodded. "Good. Something about this night makes me want one."

Packages of unopened Marlboro lights moved around the pulled kitchen drawer. She tossed Lance one. He whispered something to Nikki before exiting through the sliding door.

"You miss smoking?" Nikki said.

"Very much," Frances said. She picked a chunk of cheesecake off her hip. She didn't know where to set it, so she ate it.

"I'm really sorry, Mrs. Burnish."

"It's just a dress."

"No, about Mr. Burnish. I'm sorry."

"Well, thank you, Nikki."

Nikki grabbed one more cheesecake and exited. Frances moved closer to the sliding door, trying to see past her reflection. Outside a circular flame seemed to float as it hovered in Frances' left eye. Colleen Kellerman's face, looking plastic and cold, like a mannequin's, reflected in the sliding door next to Frances'. An enormous diamond shone on Colleen's ring finger as her hand rested on Frances' shoulder. Her instinct was to shake her hand off but didn't.

"It was a beautiful service, Frances." Impressed with Colleen's ability to lie, Frances turned, their noses almost touching. "I minored in psychology, so if you ever want to talk." She removed Colleen's hand from her shoulder, and expected to toss it aside, but held onto it when she noticed two glowing circles disappear around the corner.

"Colleen, did Milton's weight bother you? The truth. I mean, you're so particular about everything looking the same on our street. Same painted mailboxes. Same pattern of Christmas lights. Same. It's all the same."

"I did worry about my theme parties. I worried he wouldn't be able to find a costume. I worried because of that, neither of you would come."

She stared at the cheesecake stain in her reflection. She put her head on Colleen's shoulder. "His weight bothered me too."

Frances couldn't sleep. She moved to David's room, which she had made up, hoping he'd stay. He'd missed Milton's showing. Said he couldn't do the small talk. Said it hurt his ears. The day of the funeral, he arrived via a Lyft at six in the morning. He didn't bring a suitcase, just his work satchel. Instead of starting a fight, she said it was good to see him and that his father was proud of him: a tenure track at twenty-nine. Very impressive. He responded with, "Dad hated zoology." He picked up a picture of Milton eating ribs, the one the restaurant took after he beat their challenge and received a free meal. "But he loved you," Frances said. And then they sat in silence until George Scuro knocked on the door to take them to the funeral home.

The bedroom window faced the cul-de-sac. She looked over Vintage Woods Court. Everyone followed Colleen Kellerman's holiday rules. Red lights wrapped around the base of the trees, with white lights snaking through the limbs and lining the house. Everyone except Lance Reynolds. His house was lit up brilliantly colorful as if he was furloughing elves for the season.

Across the street, a front door opened. Cinna, Nikki's dog, charged out. He did his business then played in the snow. Nikki snapped for him to run back in the house. Once inside, she could see Nikki's silhouette fluttering around her room like a bird. Frances checked the time. 2:27 AM. She called David. Voicemail.

"David, it's Mom. Listen, I'm sorry we never let you have a dog. I am. But, I was allergic. Lungs shut down. Couldn't breathe." She kept her voice even as tears moved over her lips. "I'm glad you were here today. So successful. Your father would brag about you at parties. 'My son the professor' and all. He was such a softy . . . probably all that fat around him." She took in a quick breath. "Okay then. Have a good first day of class. Tell Utah I said hello. Happy January."

She held her phone to her chest and watched Nikki flap around her room until grief forced sleep.

@

Samson was a German shepherd mix. His eyes were black and sad. He was the only one at the kennel not wanting Frances' attention. "Is that one sick?" Frances asked the Humane Society volunteer.

"Traumatized. The owner died in front of him a few days ago. Heart attack. His name is Samson."

Frances repeated his name and knelt to poke her fingers through the cage. Samson sniffed and then licked them, making Frances smile. The dog stood and wagged his tail.

"That's the first signs of life I've seen from him. Poor guy cried himself to sleep last two nights."

Frances held out her hands. "I had bacon for breakfast. Same trick I used to gain affection from my husband." Frances stood, placing her hands on her hips. "Samson, do you want to come home with me. Milton hates dogs, but I don't care. My home will be your home."

"Ma'am, we want all of our animals to go to loving homes. May I ask: who is Milton."

"Oh, just my husband." Frances winked. "But don't you worry none about it. He's dead." She reached through the cage. "That's right Samson. He died and we buried him yesterday, so he no longer has a say about what I bring home, whether they be snazzy dresses or a beautiful dog or a salad." Samson barked and jumped up on the cage. Frances rubbed his head. "Consider your society one dog short."

At home, Samson sat upright as she opened the refrigerator.

"I'm afraid all we have is cheese," she said, looking down at the dog. "My husband liked cold cuts too. And spare ribs and filets and flavored jerky and bacon by the pound and butter pop-sicles. You think the neighbors could have coordinated better to pay homage." She put her head back in the fridge and pulled out a plate of meatloaf. She smelled it and then made a face at its stench. "If you can eat a live bunny, I'm sure you can handle that."

Samson hovered over the meatloaf. "It's okay. Go ahead." He ate. "Good, boy." She grabbed a beer from the refrigerator's top shelf. "It's happy hour somewhere." She twisted the cap and took a swig.

"Frances?" Collen Kellerman stood with an assorted cheese plate. "Your door was wide open." She pointed. "When did you get a dog?"

"An hour ago. Colleen. Samson. Samson. Colleen."

Samson picked his head up for a moment, then went back to the meatloaf.

"My, my. This one has an appetite that could have rivaled Milton's." Frances took a swig. "Where are my manners? Colleen, beer?"

Colleen put the cheese plate down on the kitchen island.

"It's eleven in the morning."

"And male ladybugs are called ladybugs. Now that we've exchanged facts, would you like a beer?"

Samson had pushed the meatloaf over to Colleen. The pan was empty. He looked up at her. "What does it want?"

"What do we all want?"

"Symmetry?" Colleen grinned.

"Well then, go stuff your left boob to make it as big as your right, and I'll tell Samson 'good job.'" She patted her thigh and Samson ran to her. She scratched his head and gushed compliments, then Samson rolled over and took a nap. Frances sat at the table and sipped her beer. Colleen tapped the counter with her red, acrylic nails.

"Screw it. Pour me a glass of white wine."

Frances poured her wine in a coffee cup. "In case you need to travel home."

Frances finished her beer and opened another. She was halfway through it before Colleen spoke.

"Saw you talking to Nikki Longstreth last night."

Frances nodded. "Even though it looks like she stuck her face in one of those nut and bolt bins at Lowes, she really is a pretty girl."

Colleen laughed and then took a drink and then another drink. After a short silence, she said, "What did you two talk about?"

Frances could guess where this was going. She had seen Colleen's son—who was the same age as Nikki Longstreth—walk with Nikki to the railroad tracks, nestled in the tall pines behind the cul-de-sac. It was the same place David would disappear to when he was their age, to investigate animals.

Frances shook her head. "She said something nice about Milton and ate most of the cheesecake desserts. The girl knows how to pay homage."

"Was it overkill with the cheesecake and the cheese plates? Too much dairy?"

"Perfect amount. Lance Reynolds is lactose intolerant."

"Or just intolerant." Colleen grinned, and then, with that dumb grin still on her face, she said, "Philip left me. That's why he wasn't at the funeral."

Frances wanted to ask if it was because she was having an affair with Lance Reynolds, but she figured why acknowledge public domain.

"If it wasn't for the social stigmatism of being separated, I really wouldn't care," Colleen said. "I always loved the idea of him, but I don't know if I ever actually loved Phil."

Frances moved next to her. "My husband left me too." She knocked her bottle against Colleen's coffee mug.

"That's not what I . . . I'm not trying to compare . . ." Colleen's face went blank and then a cry commandeered her entire body. Frances held her close, but still managed to drink her beer. "I know you loved Milton. I feel so sad for you. I mean, you can't control love or who you love or how you love. Stupid, dumb love."

Frances patted Colleen's back. Aside from her communist rule over the cul-de-sac, she knew very little about Colleen Kellerman, which was why she had yet to make up her mind about her. Hating men without knowing them was easy, like with Lance Reynolds, but she felt it unnatural to have snap judgments about other women.

"Milton was impossible," Frances said, still rubbing Colleen's back. "You know, I could always rely on him forgetting to do something. Weird thing to rely on, but I loved him for it. He'd get a funny look on his face and then stretch out his hands as if in cuffs, and then he'd give this look and his eyes would make him look small, like a child, and I'd laugh and hug him and tell him he was a brilliant moron." She looked at the refrigerator. No doubt that appliance would always remind her of Milton. She nodded. "I don't know if he was the great love of my life, but I loved him. Very much. He was a good partner."

"How bad does it hurt?"

"I can't believe he lived this long. His heart actually pumped the same contents as a deep fryer." Frances covered her dumb grin by drinking. "I guess in a way, I've been preparing for it for so long, I've been ready for the hurt. Now that it's here, I feel like I've already been through it. Feels like a damn rerun."

She finished her beer and grabbed another.

"I know what you mean," Colleen said, holding out her cup for more wine. "I always knew Phil would leave me for someone younger, prettier, more . . . experimental or whatever. Now that it's happened . . ." She shrugged and gulped her wine.

The doorbell rang. Samson barked and ran to the door. He jumped up and pawed the knob.

"Frances, I think your dog is actually trying to open the door."

Frances agreed and then opened it. Three packages lay on the porch.

"Chico's?" Colleen said, reading the label, judgment in her tone. She raised her hands and apologized. "I'm such a bitch."

"It's your right, as it is for all women." Frances picked up the packages. "You come back here anytime you want for more morning adult beverages." As Colleen passed the threshold, Frances said, "Phil's an idiot. I'm not saying that because he's leaving you. I'm saying that because it's a fact."

"I know," Colleen said. "But he helped me make a beautiful boy."

Colleen left. Frances weighed the packages. More funeral dresses. She opened them and put them in David's closet. She retrieved the other funeral dresses from her room and hung them next to the new ones.

"Seven funeral dresses," she said to Samson. "One for each day of the week." Samson looked at her. "Oh, come here, you." She clapped her hands and Samson reached his paws up and she put them on her shoulders so they could slow dance. "Last time

I danced David lived here. Funny how even back then I thought Milton was large, but he could still twirl me and hold me close enough to where our cheeks could touch." She hummed a tune she could no longer place and danced with her dog next to the window that David must've looked out many times, waiting for Milton to return from his business trips. Samson set his paws on the windowpane. "You know he never once checked on David. Not once. All those years and poor David must've heard him challenging the floorboards and he never even peeked in on him to show he missed his face." She offered Samson her male impression. "'Boys know fathers love their sons. No need to always show it. Makes them tough.'"

The maples lining the street now stretched over the road. When they'd first moved in, they were just sticks pretending to be trees. She sat with Samson looking out the window waiting for something to pop or rattle to disturb the house's deafening silence. She thought of the pill cases next to Milton's sink and how she'd lay in bed in the morning waiting for the snap of the case so she wouldn't have to remind Milton to take his pills.

"Samson, I saved you today. Maybe someday you'll return the favor."

Samson pawed the window and whimpered. Frances attached a leash to his collar and led him outside.

She fastened the leash to a porch post and reached into her coat for a Marlboro Light. She put the unlit cigarette in her mouth and inhaled, then exhaled, then inhaled again. Samson moved around the yard sniffing then looked at her and whimpered.

"What? This?" she said, holding up the cigarette. "Did your old owner smoke? Don't you worry. I never light it. No fire." With the mention of "fire," Samson squatted, leaving a fresh pile on the snow. "Fire," she said again, and again Samson squatted. "Remarkable."

Nikki Longstreth appeared from the woods. Her strides were quick, vanishing behind her house. Lance Reynolds also emerged, but walked in the other direction, towards the back of his house.

"Come, Samson," she said. "Best not to get involved." She yanked his leash, leading him back inside.

@

The doorbell awoke them from their naps.

"It's okay, boy. Just the door."

Colleen entered.

"Now, if you're going to have that dog, you need to clean up after it."

Frances nodded. "Gonna deem it an 'Eyesore' and give me a peephole violation, are you?"

"Don't be ridiculous. Warning first and then the citation."

She smiled, but Frances couldn't tell if she was being polite or joking.

"You signed the agreement for the cul-de-sac, Frances. Three citations and it's put to a vote whether or not to keep the dog."

"You're the only one who votes."

"Exactly."

Colleen's movements were clumsy. She waddled about the foyer. Frances grinned. Colleen went home and must've kept drinking.

She moved to the living room and ran her hand along the sofa. "Don't you think it's just awful how Lance Reynolds has women over all the time. And he's engaged too. Do you know where his fiancé is?"

"In Africa helping children with cleft palates or something."

Everyone knew this because if Lance wasn't telling people, Colleen was.

Colleen picked up a ceramic angel. "Doctor Fiancée. Doesn't she sound perfect? So perfect she told Lance to get his nastiness out of his system, so when she returns, he is to be all hers." She rubbed the angel with her thumb. "I don't get this generation and their openness. Why can't they just bottle it up and ignore its damage like we do?" She placed the angel on the edge.

"Colleen, would you like to go to church with me on Sunday?"

"What?"

"Church. Would you like to go to church with me? Milton never went. David never went. Been going by myself for . . . well . . .

Milton and I would have been married thirty-three years come April, so I guess a long time now."

"I don't believe in God," she said. "Will I burn alive or something once I enter."

"If you combust into flames upon entry, I think you'll flip-flop on God's nature real quick."

@

Milton's blood didn't circulate well the last few years, making him feel cold and the house very hot. Frances turned the thermostat down and opened a window while she drank bourbon. It smelled like a snowstorm was approaching. Nimbostratus clouds moved fast overhead. Across the street, Nikki's front door opened and Cinna, her Airedale, came charging out. Nikki held up the dog's collar. Samson saw him and wagged his tail.

"Let's go say hi."

Cinna charged at Samson. Both dogs balanced on their hind legs and pawed and played in the street. Nikki ran over to Frances.

"I gotta get this collar on him or Mrs. Kellerman will yell at me."

"Oh, you don't worry about her. Let the dogs play."

"I read online that Airedales don't train well. I have to take the collar off inside or he tries to eat it." She grinned. "But look at him. He looks like a cartoon, something fantastical." Nikki wasn't wearing a coat, just an oversized sweatshirt that stopped at her bare thighs. She hugged herself to keep warm. "Wait. When did you get a dog?"

"Samson's his name. This morning."

"I got Cinna after Mom left. She hated dogs."

"Milton did too." She dug a cigarette from her jacket and put it in her mouth. "Cinna's a fun name."

"We read *Julius Caesar* last year. There's this poet named Cinna. Angry townspeople want to tear him apart because they think he's one of the conspirators who killed Caesar, but he's not. He's just a poet. Then the townspeople kill him anyway for his bad poetry."

"Why?"

She shrugged. "Trying to find solace in something they didn't even know made them sad." The big sweatshirt slid down her left shoulder, revealing a pink lace bra strap.

Cinna chased a squirrel into Lance Reynolds' yard.

"Want to know a sad fact, Mrs. Burnish?"

"Make me feel young. Call me Frances." She winked. "What's the sad fact?"

"It's what I learned from *Caesar*. We want to be fooled by something that will destroy us. And here's the sad part," she looked at Lance Reynolds' house, "when we discover what it is—the thing that will destroy us—that's usually when we choose to, like, lean into it and welcome its destruction."

Cinna squatted leaving a pile on Lance's lawn. Nikki took a paper bag out of her sweatshirt front pocket. Frances put her arm out.

"Leave that one."

"Frances, can I ask you a question?"

"Shoot."

"You ever go online? Not to like shop or whatever, but to like, talk to people?" Nikki shook her head, not giving Frances a chance to answer. "People are weird." She paused as if thinking about a specific thing. "I mean, like totally weird."

"Online. Offline. That doesn't change."

Cinna ran back towards the house and through the open door. Nikki waved and started back to her house.

"Can I buy some pot?"

"What?"

Frances pretended her cigarette was a joint. "Pot. Can I buy some?"

Nikki walked back to her. "Start with this."

She pulled a joint from the sweatshirt's pouch pocket. Frances stuck it behind her ear like she used to do in college when she and her girlfriends drove around town. "What do I owe you?"

"Like any good dealer would say . . . the first one's on me."

A few days later Frances returned home from a dinner with a friend and there was another package. More clothing. Frances set it down in her closet. She was about to open it but noticed Milton's sweater vests. He hadn't worn them in years. She pressed a burgundy one to her face; somehow it still smelled of musty wool and stir-fry; she slipped it over her head and modeled it for Samson who was lying on the floor in her bedroom. She ran her hand over the extra fabric, pressing it against her stomach.

"I'm worried the only thing I will remember about Milton is his size."

She put the sweater back on the hanger and took the package to David's room. Five more outfits from Chico's hung next to her funeral dresses, below them was a delivery from Talbots she'd forgotten to open. Digging her phone from her pocket, she lay on the closet floor and called David. Voicemail.

"You remember Janie Lorenz? My old sorority sister? She missed the funeral so she took me to dinner tonight—if you can call Red Robin at the mall dinner." Her voice went high. Samson moved to her feet. "So there we are, at Red Robin in Tuttle Mall—which is becoming a virtual crime zone—and she proceeds to tell me how she met a nice guy online—Doug. She says he's so different from Harry—her still alive ex-husband—and that's a good thing. Then—get this, David—she puts down her fork—only psychos order a salad at Red Robin—reaches across the table and pats my hand, a real condescending pat too, and says, 'You'll meet your Doug soon enough.' Imagine it now. All these years Janie Lorenz was out there reinventing what it means to be a bitch." She paused. "No plane crashes made the news, so I assume you are safe and sound in Utah."

She moved to the window and sat down. Christmas lights spirited the street. She tried not to look at Lance's house, but couldn't help it. The lit reindeer and dancing elves and colored lights and Santa on the roof commanded her gaze.

"Janie Lorenz. Janie Lorenz. Janie Lorenz." She huffed. "I swear, you share one story with someone years ago and that is seen as the golden nugget of truth after thirty plus years of marriage." Samson put his front paws on her lap. She stared at that stupid Santa on Lance's stupid house.

"I wish it'd rain and wash this snow away, along with the season." She entered her closet, made a bed with Milton's clothes, and fell asleep next to Samson. She dreamed of brisket.

@

Frances had already finished half the joint before Colleen honked. She'd put on one of her new outfits from Chico's for church. Colleen gushed over her outfit as Frances entered her SUV. "I didn't know church was so fancy. My goodness. You make me want to go home and change to let the girls out before the Lord."

Colleen declared that she was one of those people that didn't play music during car rides. She did have a CD sticking out of the player, but acted oddly and tossed it in the backseat when Frances suggested it. It landed up: *How Not to Be a Victim.*

"Do you think it's weird that Nikki Longsteth serves tables at George Scuro's restaurant? You have to be nineteen to serve alcohol. She's seventeen."

"Nikki looks twenty-three and talks like she's earning her masters in philosophy. Besides, I think George is just doing something nice for her. Must have been hard after her mom left." She rubbed her face. It felt like someone else's hands were touching her face, or maybe, her hands were touching someone else's face.

"Is church interactive? What if the minister calls on me? In college, if the professor called on students I would drop the class and find one where the professor just lectured."

Frances laughed. "If you get called on, please answer."

"No."

"I don't know what you will say, but I promise it will be my new favorite thing. Please answer."

"You're stoned."

"So?"

Colleen laughed and then Frances laughed and their smiles filled the silence. Then Colleen said, "Wait? You're really stoned? I was kidding."

"Put that CD in. I fear I may need to sober up."

Frances usually sat in the back at church, but she led Colleen to the front row, before the massive picture of the crucifixion above the altar. The minister gave Frances a sympathetic look. Frances responded by pointing to herself and then waving it off as if it was no big deal.

Frances enjoyed church stoned. The music sounded better. Passing the collection plate was fun. Greeting her neighbor was a tactile wonder. During the sermon, Frances reached over and petted Colleen's long dark hair. It was soft, the opposite of Ginny Scuro's. Suddenly she worried Ginny Scuro's medically induced emotional prison would be permanent. She stood.

"Minister Allan, you said after a tragedy God helps us recoup as if we are plants and God is the sun or something. I mean, Christ, all of a sudden religion is photosynthesis." The congregation gasped. Frances swatted Colleen's hand away. "At Milton's funeral, you quoted Psalm 132, verse 13." She cleared her throat, and swept her arms out wide, striking a pose that mimicked the minister. "*For the Lord has chosen Zion; He has desired it for His dwelling place.*" She shook her head. "Does anyone know what that means?"

The minister stepped down from the altar. "Frances. You're mourning. Please, wait for me in my office."

"I'm not mourning. Not yet. Milton was on businesses trips longer than he's been dead." She appreciated her own argument and gave herself a high-five.

"Frances, please." The minister smiled at the congregation.

The beautiful colors in the stained glass window reflected the sun.

"Psalm 132? No one? Well, I think it means that God sees Himself as some hotshot afterlife real estate mogul. He took the last lot available and awards us free rent as long as we buy into His mysticism." She looked over the congregation. "Classic narcissist." She grinned and looked at Colleen. "Let's get pancakes."

Reverend Allan held out his hands. There was no admonishment in his gesture, just empathy and forgiveness. Frances smiled. Despite his incompetence, she'd always liked him. He had a nice face and copious patience. She stepped to him and inter-locked her arm through his, her voice light and rhythmic. "I've always preferred Isaiah chapter 62, verse 1: *For Zion's sake I will not keep silent, and for Jerusalem's sake I will not be quiet, until her righteousness goes forth as brightness, and her salvation as a burning torch.*" She pointed at the orange crafted sun between large open palms on the stained glass window. "We can't trust Zion because we have no idea what happens next. I suppose the city on the hill will have just as much nonsense and pain there as it does here. I mean, it's not like management's changed." She moved to her tiptoes and whispered in the reverend's ear. "Ask me why I wield my own torch of salvation."

"Why do you wield your own torch of salvation?"

"Good question. Because *I* lit it." She winked. "Go team!"

In Colleen's car, Frances howled with laughter. Colleen's laugh was lower but just as joyous. They laughed until they had no breath.

"Same time next week?" Colleen said.

This time tears streamed down their faces and they laughed until they hurt. Frances grabbed Colleen's arm as her breathing slowed.

"What was that all about?" Colleen asked.

"I'm sad. I'm angry. I'm stoned."

"So you really are stoned?"

"So, so stoned. Nikki Longstreth gave me a joint. Smoked it this morning. Very good. Much better than I remember. Botany has improved since the seventies."

Colleen squeezed the steering wheel.

"I'm jealous of her. Jealous of Nikki Longstreth. I mean, crazy jealous."

Frances petted Colleen's cheek. "Me too."

"Why are you jealous of her?"

"She's young. She has so much time to figure out her pain. I felt like I was in hibernation. I never even considered my pain until I heard Milton fall out of bed when his heart quit him. Now I'm just backlogged with pain. Awoken to it." She shrugged. "The simplicity of a content life numbs us to dormant voices."

"You are pretty damn poetic when you're stoned."

They watched cars pass by the church.

"It's supposed to storm today."

Frances nodded and suggested they get home before the snow started.

Big flakes hit the windshield once they turned into The Estate of Tall Pines. Although Colleen lived two houses over, she pulled into Frances' driveway.

"Want to do something?" Colleen asked.

Frances shook her head. "I need to let my dog out."

Her footprints marked the snow's dusting. She looked back as she opened her front door. Colleen was crying. She waved Colleen inside.

Frances opened the refrigerator and grabbed a piece of Gouda. She poured two bourbons and the ladies watched Samson chomp at snow in the backyard. Darkness came with the storm.

"I don't drink straight bourbon," Colleen said.

Frances prompted Colleen to raise her glass.

"To new things." She laughed at Colleen's disgust. "Wanna see something neat?" Frances opened the sliding door. "Samson. Fire!"

Samson squatted and left a pile. Frances pointed. "I'm not cleaning that up."

Colleen laughed and tried another sip and coughed. "Smooth."

Frances knocked on the glass and Samson came running. He stood on the mat while she dried him with a dishtowel.

"Milton hated dogs. Just hated them. So, I lied to David when he was a boy. Said I had a dog allergy so we couldn't get one."

"Why?"

"Couldn't stand to see David angry at Milton for one more thing."

Droplets had scattered across the floor. Samson took a step and slipped, scratching the hardwood. Frances dropped to her knees and rubbed the marked wood.

"It won't come out. It won't come out." Samson licked her face. "Now, I know you didn't mean to, but back when Milton was more agile, he put this hardwood floor in himself. He was very proud of it. Very proud."

Frances grabbed her bourbon and walked to her front porch. She plugged in her Christmas lights. Now Nikki's house was the only house not lit. She took a sip and looked over her neighborhood. Colleen stood next to her with the door open.

"Longstreth's missed the light curfew. Go do what you need to do."

"The Peephole doesn't need me tonight. Just going to enjoy my drink."

"Good for you."

They both seemed to focus on the darkness of Nikki's house.

"So why are you all invested in Nikki?"

"What do you mean?" Colleen's voice went high.

"You said jealousy. I sensed something else."

Colleen shrugged and swallowed the rest of her bourbon. A squirrel tight-roped the porch's banister. It stopped before Frances and stood on its hind legs.

"Maybe it's a sign from Milton. Did he like squirrels?" Colleen said.

Frances shook her head. "Said they had a bland taste."

The women laughed bringing Samson to the door. A car turned onto the court. Its headlights splashed over the squirrel. Samson charged at the rodent, chasing it to the street.

Car brakes screeched.

Colleen grabbed Frances' arm. Frances sucked in a deep breath.

The car had swerved into the Longstreth's lawn, carving mud tracks ten yards deep.

Nikki swung open the car door and threw up her hands.

"I didn't see him. Oh my God, I didn't see him."

Frances walked to the front of the porch, sucking in her breath.

Hysterics controlled Nikki. She turned to Frances. "I'm so sorry! I didn't see him."

Samson ran from behind the car and back to the house.

Frances pointed. "For heaven's sakes, go help that poor girl."

Nikki's mascara bled like crude oil down her face. Samson lay at her feet. Frances set a cup of hot cocoa on the table.

"I didn't see him, Mrs. Burnish. I mean, I almost . . ."

"Call me, Frances."

Frances handed Nikki a cup of cocoa and told her to drink up. Nikki continued to cry but Frances raised the mug to her face and made her choose between crying and cocoa. "Sorry," she said, licking the cocoa off her lips.

"Don't apologize to me, apologize to Frau Kellerman. Those tire tracks really tainted the symmetry of the Peephole. Isn't that right, Colleen."

Nikki's eyes went wide, sucking in her breath. Colleen burst into laughter and Frances followed suit. Nikki grinned, taking another sip of cocoa.

"Kiddo, I should be thanking you. You didn't kill my dog." She looked at Samson and shook her head. "Risked it all for a squirrel. Tsk. Tsk. So much for remarkable." Frances scratched Samson's head, stood and hovered over Nikki. "You're a hero." She stared at Nikki's head, then buried her free hand into Nikki's scalp as if checking for a tick. Nikki's eyes bulged. "Hold this." Frances gave Nikki her bourbon so she could use both hands to root around in her hair. "Why would you take your beautiful blonde hair and dip it in sludge? And what's with this pink stripe? All these chemicals will make you bald."

Nikki looked away. "My mom's hair was blonde." She looked at Colleen. "Like yours used to be."

"Yeah," Frances said. "Why do you dye your hair, black?"

Colleen palmed her dark hair as she finished her bourbon. She walked to the bottle for a refill. She drank the new pour like a shot. "I'm afraid if I answer that question I won't know when I'll stop talking." She poured another drink and leaned against the island.

After a silence, Frances laughed. "Aren't we just generations of sadness." She continued to laugh as she spoke. "Nikki, unscrew that shit out of your face. Colleen, grab the bourbon. Girls, you're coming with me."

She led them upstairs, to David's closet. She opened it revealing her funeral dresses. "In case they had to bury his big ass in parts on different days." Colleen laughed and couldn't stop. She took a swig from the bottle and gave it to Frances who did the same. "You don't have time to mourn at a funeral. Everyone wants to give their condolences. You have to listen to their pity and their sympathy and how they will miss the dead. All a funeral is, is hosting a party you never wanted to throw." She offered Nikki the bottle. "A vice for a vice." Nikki took a gulp. She coughed and it spilled on her chin.

Frances told Nikki to take the piercings out of her face. "You too, Colleen. Wash off all that make-up. Time for a fashion show. Every now and then we need something new, because the old stuff, no matter where we are, no matter what we wear, no matter what lies we tell ourselves, the old stuff is always with us. Acting like it isn't just broadcasts stupidity."

Frances lingered in the hallway as the girls washed their faces. She thought of Ginny Scuro all alone in her house and told them she'd be back. She attached the leash to Samson's collar, saying she learned her lesson, and went outside.

Big heavy flakes fell. Samson danced on the porch, wanting to play in it. Snow twinkled before the colored Christmas lights that outlined Lance Reynolds' entire house. Wreaths decorated with red bulbs hung outside each window. Lit reindeer were grazing in his front lawn. Lance Reynolds' perfect house perfectly celebrated the perfect season and belonged on a perfect postcard to advertise its perfection.

She stood at the base of Ginny's driveway. How could Ginny sleep with Lance Reynolds' house lit up like hellfire? Frances bent down and packed snow tight and round. She stopped midway in Lance's driveway and thought of the one time Milton played catch with David. She took out her phone and called him.

"Hello, Mom. I—"

"David, hold on one moment. I'm about to do something wildly wonderful."

She set the phone down and squared her shoulders, taking aim at Lance's front door. She looked at the woods, the ones where she saw Lance and Nikki returning. She now had a reason to hate him. She now had a reason to like Colleen. She now had a day to tell Ginny to rival her manic episodes. She held the leash with her left and palmed the snowball with her right. Samson crouched and wagged his tail in anticipation. She threw the snowball. Direct hit. Lance's front porch light turned on. Samson barked. The door opened. Samson ran forward, stretching the leash taut, until she let go.

# Falling Away

THE MID-FEBRUARY WINDS swirled wrappers and plastic cups across the faded yellow lines of the parking lot. George Scuro had gone outside, away from The Florentine's kitchen, to listen to his wife's message. This was only the second time she'd called since he'd moved out in December. As he punched in his voicemail code, he grimaced at the 'No Deliveries between 11 and 2' sign posted by the door. Today alone three different deliverymen had ignored it. *Goddamn Apple Chicanery. The most overlooked font.* Per usual, his wife's message started mid-thought. "Not like this. Not a message on the phone. You call me, George! You call me back!" The familiar mania in her voice popped in non-rhythmic crescendos reminding him of all those sleepless nights fraught with limitless concern. But now, with his boys out of her house, and safe, he didn't need to listen to her, not anymore. He held the power button down and watched the screen go black.

A gust of wind sent his hands into his pockets. Soon enough itchy eczema bumps would surface, cracking his skin at the knuckles. A stray dog walked down the alley sniffing for food. It caught a wrapper and licked the dried cheese stuck to its corner. It gave George a cold and desperate look. He shrugged. "Sorry, boy." Back inside, he pushed away a time he would have scooped up the mutt and given it a home.

The wind blew the heavy security door shut, a violent, final slam, reminding George to get lost in the frenzy of Valentine's

Day dinner rush. He got word to those working the phones not to bother him if his wife called—ex-wife. "Just leave her on hold." He didn't need to give a reason. They understood.

Holding a food ticket, he plated trays. Normally, he'd be out front schmoozing with his customers since half of them came in just to see him. George was a showman, affable and charming, with tantalizing stories and a deft ability to crack one-liners with such ease, and even when his words were a repeat, it was somehow funnier the second time. This helped the customers think The Florentine was their special place, making the suburbanites of Columbus feel celebrated for coming all the way downtown to dine. But tonight, he just wanted to rotate the ticket wheel.

"Nikki! Nikki, your order's up. It's dying here! First, you were late to work, now this! Not a good night for you, Nikki. Let's go, let's go!"

Nikki Longstreth ran over, holding a tray of salads, her blue hair invaded by blonde roots. A swollen redness surrounded a silver ring pinching her bottom lip. Other than the ears, it was against the server's dress code to have facial piercings.

"Being late wasn't my fault. I was helping Mrs. Burnish find her dog. It ran like three streets over and wouldn't come home." She tongued the ring in her lip. "Guess some old dude was having a heart attack or something and Mrs. Burnish's dog, like, totally sensed this, and stood over him on the sidewalk and just barked and barked and barked until someone called 9-1-1." She paused. "Dog's like a super-hero or something."

"Mrs. Burnish has a dog?" This was all George could think to say.

Nikki nodded like it was common knowledge. George had shared a property line with the Burnishes for over two decades and they never had a pet, and as he recalled, Frances Burnish hated dogs, was deathly allergic to them. His wife said they couldn't get a dog out of fear Frances would never visit. George looked at the ticket again. "Why are you working out of your station?"

"I had to take two of Peg's tables. These are the salads for twenty-two. They aren't ready for their food. I'm in the weeds bad."

"Peg only has a three-table section tonight. This means you have seven tables and Peg only has one?" Nikki nodded. "Does Peg look okay to you? Her eyes? Do they look . . . normal?"

Nikki shrugged. "Same as always, I guess."

George examined the plates of spaghetti in his hands. From sitting under the heat lamp so long the sauce had solidified, looking like a fungal film.

"I'll take care of this. Apologize to the table. Offer them free dessert—one of the homemade pies. And Nikki, after the shift, we need to talk about that thing in your lip." Nikki nodded, then exited back into the fray of the dinner rush.

He hired Nikki before he'd moved away from Vintage Woods Court. Over the summer Nikki's mother had left her and her father for some cult. Well, George wasn't sure if it was actually a cult, but that's the word Nikki's father had used, so he used it too. George's mother had died when he was young, so he knew what it was like to suddenly not have a mom, and he wanted to do something for Nikki, create a healthy distraction, so he offered her a job. "You have to be nineteen to serve alcohol in Ohio, so don't tell," he'd said. Nikki was only sixteen at the time, but she looked much older, something about the pain in her eyes. "Some secrets are okay if they don't hurt anyone," he added, hoping to make her feel like she was part of something important.

After the dinner rush, George sat in his office, swiveling in a leather chair as old as the restaurant. He had yet to find the time to take down the pictures of his wife pinned to the corkboard behind the desk. Maybe he'd misjudged her tone earlier. Maybe Ginny was lucid today. Maybe she just missed him on Valentine's Day. But he knew better. The day he moved out, Ginny's eyes seemed to flood with happiness, as if the synapses in her brain wasn't the problem, but he was.

He unpinned a photo of her holding Adam while pregnant with Liam and thought of her message: *Not like this. Not a message on the phone. You call me, George! You call me back!* Urgency controlled her voice. He laughed. Most likely she'd yet to take down the Christmas decorations. The homeowners' association required all lights to be down by mid-January. That's all it was. She had received an orange sheet, a notice of non-compliance— an "Eyesore"—from the dictator of the Peephole. Yes, that's all it was, nonsense, like all her manic episodes. He dropped the photo in the trash.

There was a knock. Peg slumped against the office door. Her eyes red. Her painted eyebrows gone. "Pete took me off the schedule next week." She wiped her face and stepped towards him. "I had a bad night is all, George. The new meds for my foot pain have me a bit loopy, but I'll be fine come Monday. You'll see. Could you talk to Pete? Get me back my usual shifts?"

Peg had served her first table at The Florentine in the seventies. A year ago, her fortieth year there, *Columbus Alive* published an article about her dedication to the restaurant. In the article, Peg said the most wonderful things about him, Ginny, the boys, and his father, saying she felt part of the Scuro clan. A framed copy of the article sat on the shelf in front of him, a present from Peg.

"You haven't been yourself, Peg. Serving is a young person's game. You'll be seventy this year."

"I need to pay the bills." She paused, most likely to give him time to think of the bad investment she'd made with her brother a few years back. Her brother had taken Peg for thirty thousand. "Besides, I love this place, Georgie. You know that. I'd do anything for it. I'd never quit on you."

She called him Georgie when he was a kid, but now she only said it to remind him of their history, to remind him that, once, she had trained him.

He unlocked the safe and counted out bills.

"No, sir. I will not ask for a loan like all the other riff-raff through the years. The day your mother died, Betty Winegate asked your father for money to pay her rent. And we all know she spent it on vodka. I won't be a part of that history. No, sir."

After he'd counted out two thousand dollars, he put it in a manila envelope.

"It's not a loan, Peg."

He held out the envelope, looking down, not wanting to see her reaction.

"Sometimes things just end."

Nikki was wiping down the salad bar as Peg stormed by. George waved her in. She plodded forward, keeping her gaze to the floor.

"What does your father think of that thing in your lip?"

"He doesn't know. Did it at a stoplight on my way here."

"You what?"

Nikki shrugged. "That thing with Mrs. Burnish's dog really freaked me out. And then after I found the dog, Mrs. Burnish was being so nice to me. Like really nice. And it's not the first time she'd been like that with me. I don't like it when she's so nice."

"Why?"

She shrugged. "She was talking about my mom, Mr. Scuro. *My mom.* Saying how if she could see me now with how helpful and how beautiful I was, and then she said no God can compete with the love of a child and . . ." Nikki looked up as she trailed off, widening her eyes, fighting off tears. "So, on the way here, I shoved a needle in my face."

He sighed. "You need to take it out—not because of the dress code for the floor—but because it looks infected. Come here." He motioned her closer. She winced when he touched her lip. He snapped his fingers twice then opened his hand. She unclasped the silver ring and dropped it in his palm. Dried pus and blood stuck to it.

"How much did the ring cost?"

She told him. George reached into his pocket and dug out the cost of the ring. He guided her into the kitchen and opened the First Aid Kit. He tipped the bottle of antiseptic over a napkin and put it on Nikki's lip. She recoiled. "Bad ideas usually result in pain, kiddo. I swear, just when I want to brag how smart you are, you do something like this." She laughed. He poured antiseptic on another napkin and handed it to her. He told her to hold it over the hole in her lip for a few minutes and then to rinse her mouth out with saltwater.

"Saltwater?"

"If you don't follow these orders you'll need your bottom lip amputated. No one brags about how nice their gums look."

The way she looked at him reminded him of Adam holding an assault rifle outside Kabul. Both Adam and Liam had acted aggressively to the divorce. Liam only came home for Christmas during college winter break and a month later George received the picture of Adam holding the assault rifle—Adam's way of telling him he'd reenlisted.

"Go finish your side work so you can get home before midnight for once. Don't worry your father any more than you have to."

George shut the office door and turned on the eleven o'clock news. He'd gotten into a fearful habit of listening to the news because sometimes if a local soldier died in active duty, it was the lead story. Tonight's lead story reported on the continued local coyote sightings in suburbia. A few cats and dogs had gone missing and the coyotes were the assumed culprits. The anchorman warned parents to keep small children and pets in their homes after dark. When Adam was thirteen and Liam was eight, George took them camping in southern Ohio. They joked that it was an expedition to find the Ohio Grassman, Ohio's version of Bigfoot. In the middle of the night, George jarred from a dead sleep. Adam was already awake. His keen instinct for sensing danger made him a light sleeper even then. His right index finger pressed against his lips and his left index finger pointed to his ear. Subtle rapid footsteps circled the tent. Adam mouthed "coyotes" and then turned the lantern to its highest beam. Canine silhouettes rose giant against the tent's orange nylon. Adam said, "Let's feed them Liam." George laughed and the footsteps scampered away. After Adam had fallen back asleep, George marveled at his son's awareness. He himself had no survival instinct and felt insignificant knowing he had nothing to teach his son on the subject.

Nikki stood in the doorway, her light blue Florentine tee untucked and stained with red sauce. There were three waiters on the front of the shirt, representing the three generations of the family. He had the shirts made back when he thought the boys were interested in the business. Nikki slipped her jacket over the shirt. "Mr. Scuro, could you walk me to my car? Nick and Pete are playing cards up front and I don't want to bother them."

He widened his eyes. He must've fallen asleep. Something he used to catch his father doing while taking inventory at the end of the night. He looked at his phone and thought about turning it back on, but didn't. He yawned, grabbed his coat, and walked Nikki outside.

"There was a woman in my station tonight. She said she was friends with you, but there was something about the way she said it that made me think she was lying. She wanted to see you, but I said you weren't in." She paused. "You didn't look like you wanted to be bothered tonight." Then added. "Valentine's Day sucks."

"You're smart, kiddo. You want to run this place when I retire? I don't think my boys have much interest. Had this woman asked Liam if she could see me, he would've led her back to the office and pointed to where I keep the checkbook. He has no understanding of this place." He looked up to the starless sky. "I'm sure she was just a sales rep from somewhere, trying to catch me off guard on a busy night. You did good."

In the distance, a glass bottle rolled against the asphalt. Nikki flinched. He pointed to a police car. He fed CPD free meals to keep them in the parking lot on the weekends after closing. An animal moved into the shadows in the alley across the street. He thought it was the dog again, but he couldn't be sure.

"She was real pretty."

He held the door open as Nikki got into her car.

"Who was?"

"The woman who asked about you. She was real pretty. Good tipper, too. Said her name was Alice."

"Alice?"

A scream echoed in the distance.

"Yeah. Why? You know her?"

His nod slipped into a headshake. "Not anymore." He offered Nikki a sad smile. "Please don't drive the backstreets this late at night. I know it's quicker, but it's not safe."

"Yes, sir, Father-Number-Two."

He didn't mind her sarcasm. He actually liked it.

"And watch out for coyotes."

"What?"

"Nothing."

She drove away, making a left towards the freeway. He waved and continued to wave long after she was gone. He conjured an image of Alice laughing, lying on the hotel bed, saying she was a creature of the night. Then she howled, and kept howling until George moved on top of her. A breeze kicked up. He itched his wrist, knowing it would make it red and bumpy. He walked back to the entrance. The wind slammed the door so hard it popped back open. He looked out into the cold, still night and howled. It felt so good he howled again.

"Boss-man, what are you doing?"

Pete and Nick wore their coats. The front room must be cleaned and locked.

"Were you howling?"

George shrugged.

"Yelling into the night, looking for a mate on Valentine's Day? I can dig it," Pete said.

"Speaking of which, there was a lady looking for you earlier," Nick said, smiling.

Pete and Nick high-fived.

Alice was making the rounds. He hadn't seen her since a food show in Toledo last summer. Since he'd moved out, he thought about that weekend and Alice's laugh, and how they both felt undeniably connected often.

"How many times did my wife call?"

Pete held up seven fingers, then he crossed his index fingers, then he held up seven fingers again.

"That might be a record," George said.

"It's not," Nick said.

"Huh," George said, wondering about all the times over the years his employees had protected him from her ridiculous intrusions.

After a silence, Nick and Pete moved to the door and George stepped aside. Nick howled and turned to George and smiled.

"See you tomorrow, boss," Nick said, not looking back.

"Tomorrow," George said, trying to wish away the unrelenting schedule of running a restaurant. He sat down in that old office chair. A place he had chosen many times over his family. He'd missed sporting events, friends' weddings, dealing with home improvements, homework questions, cul-de-sac parties, his wife's relapses . . . he'd missed so much. His fingers slid over the familiar cracks in the chair's burgundy leather. He closed his eyes. Alice had auburn hair. She smelled of eucalyptus. She explored him with more purpose than Ginny ever did. But he didn't care about any of that. Only her laugh. Her guttural, heavy laugh that seemed to play like a familiar song beckoning him to dance. That's how he felt when the boys were young and Ginny never missed her meds. Those days he'd never sit in this chair after a shift. Those days he'd speed home.

When the chair stopped spinning he opened his eyes. It took him a second to adjust to the scene. He stared at the empty space on the wall where he'd removed the picture of pregnant Ginny holding Adam. He turned on his phone. No new messages. He went to dig the picture out of the trash, but the kitchen crew had already tossed it. He grabbed his coat and headed for the door. He momentarily entertained looking for that dog, but an unexpected snowfall guided him to his car.

Habit led him the wrong way. The moment he pulled into The Estates of Tall Pines he remembered he didn't live there anymore, but he still drove to Vintage Woods Court. He parked in front of his old house. It was snowing harder now. Two houses down, at the front of the cul-de-sac, there was a For Sale sign in the yard. He smiled. The old coot was moving. Howard Havenshaw was a Vietnam veteran who had influenced Adam to enlist when he was eighteen. Ginny hated him—so did George—but Ginny hated him with percolating violence that George feared would manifest into action. *That had to be why she was calling. Howard Havenshaw would be gone forever and she needed George to know.* Content, he drove away from his old home, away from the non-decorated trees, and took the back roads to his apartment.

The snowfall demanded attention to the roads. Every few years a high school kid got himself killed driving too fast on the country roads. Once, Adam was with a friend who had crashed his car into a ditch, trying to take a curve at eighty. No one was hurt, which was a miracle, considering the damage done to the Ford Fusion. While hugging his son, he screamed at him, terrified of a world without him.

The blue radio lights distracted him, so he turned off NPR. The crunching of the snow beneath the tires folded into the darkness. He felt like he was in a different time. The back of his wrist flared with an eczema itch so he eased off the gas to scratch it. His fingers felt wet. He'd attacked his own skin until he bled. He reached into his glove compartment for a napkin when something stumbled into the road and collapsed. Slamming the breaks skidded the car into the other lane. The animal's brownish fur looked white against the headlights as it lay in the snow-covered street. George smeared his bloody fingers against his beige pea-coat. Three coyotes jumped out from the darkness and converged on the one that had collapsed. George pressed the horn, scaring them off into the darkness, where they realigned, their eyes glowing, watching, only yards away from his door.

The coyote tried to limp away. It moved down the center of the road, away from the car. Its emaciated body shone in the head-lights. Its slow gait tracked in the snow. The others had probably turned against it for food. He knew what would happen if he drove around it.

He inched the car forward, trailing it. The coyote sensed the Subaru Forester following, stopped, and turned. Its eyes didn't look like those of a predator, but of something defenseless, something stuck in this place, something lost. The eye shine along the roadside moved with them. He rolled down his window and screamed for them to get lost, to scram. They didn't move.

A vibration hummed against his thigh, knocking against Nikki's lip ring in his pocket. Ginny's ringtone. The light from the screen showed his bloodstained fingers. He silenced the phone. The news of the neighbor moving away could wait. The coyote collapsed again, its chest heaving. He could save the coyote. Yes, he could put it in the back of his Forester and save it.

He held down the horn until the glowing eyes in the woods disappeared. He opened his car door and stepped out. A bright star shone above him. Or was it too bright for a star? It must be a planet. Mercury maybe. A memory of Adam sitting in the snow at twelve, picking up a frozen cardinal, flashed liked a popping ember.

A beep. Missed call. One bar in the right corner of the phone blinked—his battery dying. A hollowness assailed him. He looked at the coyote, the undulations of its breathing became more violent. He stepped into the headlights, casting a shadow over the canine. Again, his wife's ringtone played. He wanted to tell her what he was about to do, that he was out of the office chair, that he was about to scoop up a coyote and save it, that this was who he was now, but before he could answer, the phone died.

Brandishing his dead phone, he did a three-sixty, searching for glowing eyes, listening for footsteps, ready to scream. He stepped forward, into his own shadow, towards the still coyote. It had a jagged scar across its face. He knelt, his knees now wet in the snow, and touched its head. The coyote licked his bloody hand, but the stain stayed. "It's okay, boy. It's okay." He scooped his arms under the injured animal, but this jarred it to its feet. It snarled. "I want to help. It's okay." Eye shimmer lined the road. George stepped forward, and the coyote ran off, beyond the glowing eyes, into the darkness. The eyes chased it.

George stepped away from the headlights, to the threshold of the woods. Faint rustling dissipated to silence. He shoved his hands in his pocket, touching the phone. A slow warm heat burned from his gut, flooding him with a terminal worry—*Ginny had already told him about Howard Havenshaw*. With Mercury watching, he stepped into the woods and howled, and he'd continue to howl long after the coyote didn't return and long after his headlights dimmed.

# Masquerade

ZAK TURNER STARED from his bedroom window.

Two houses down, at the apex of the cul-de-sac, Lance Reynolds, wearing only silk pajama bottoms, escorted a red-head—no doubt full from orgasms—to her dirty sedan. Although engaged—not to the redhead—Lance Reynolds had become infa-mous for his dalliances, which the neighbors seemed to forgive, as if fucking all the twenty-somethings in the 614-area code was a side-effect from being so damn handsome. Zak had seen that handsome realtor face plastered on numerous park benches and COTA busses throughout the city, pre-maturely percolating the sexual curiosity of tween girls all over greater Columbus.

"I don't get it." Zak's fist hit the window.

The redhead looked towards him. She was not Lance Reynolds' usual fare. She beamed a trashy incandescence and looked closer to forty than thirty. Her exaggerated sensual movements were not fit for the shiny suburban cage that was Vintage Woods Court. "I love you." Zak pressed his hand against the window. Ever since he stuck his finger in Brandine Hilliard on the back of the bus in the seventh grade, he had a fetish for simple, skinny girls loaded with a verbal arsenal of double negatives and subject-verb disagreement. He blocked out his wife's request for a baby and wished to lick the back of the redhead's thigh, to sneak her into the bathroom at Winter Homecoming, to help her with Algebra, to make eye contact with her until she sat down next to him on the bus, to keep going backward in life until it became simple.

An Internet redhead doppelganger still couldn't get him going. He looked down. Pathetic. Soft and rubbery, like a Vienna sausage. The doctor's hand had been clumsy with his circumcision so the folded skin was crooked, half rolling up on the left side of the tip, never a chance to be beautiful. He zipped up and cleared the history on the computer and typed in Careerbuilder.com, leaving the laptop open to a split screen between job possibilities and the article his wife e-mailed him.

@

He was playing *Resident Evil* on his PS4 when Celia entered, talking on her phone. She was excited and polite. Zak changed his weapon from a shotgun to a flame flower.

"Yes. Tomorrow then," Celia said, walking into the room.

A zombie grabbed the leg of his avatar. He set it on fire and watched it burn.

"Ten-thirty is perfect." She said goodbye and set her cell on the coffee table. After Zak didn't acknowledge her, she moved in front of the television. Zombies feasted on him. *You Died* dripped in red on the screen.

"Lance Reynolds will be here at ten-thirty tomorrow. That's A.M."

Zak pushed the controller's toggle to the left hoping it would make his wife move.

"We're putting our house on the market? Moving back to the city?"

She sucked in a breath. "I called Lance to see if he knew any contractors and it turns out he is a consultant for one. He's our neighbor, so I don't want to use him, but I do want an initial estimate."

Zak looked at the bare wall blocking the kitchen. Except for the dining room, which still had its original wall-papered-pattern of blue squares trapping gold flowers, nothing decorative hung on the walls.

"Why do you want that wall down so badly?"

"Are you serious?" She twirled and pointed at the entire space on the first floor. "We wouldn't feel so compartmentalized, so cut-off. It's suffocating here." She sauntered about. "Now you see me . . ." she moved to the kitchen, "and now you don't."

For years they lived in a loft downtown. One big open square. Everywhere was their bedroom, and that's how they acted.

A cork popped. She returned with a glass of white wine. She took a sip and then another and then another.

"What did you think of the article?" He started a new game. "It doesn't mention drugs at all. Not even herbal alternatives."

He could tell she had read it too many times. Her voiced changed, capturing the cadence he'd heard while she took a work call. "Their study targets the distinct connection between virility and personal successes in both work and love." She paused. "You liked your old job once. Maybe that's how you'd feel about a new job."

For a decade Zak had toted different drugs to different hospitals to different doctors just to have the same conversation, and the predictability of the job manifested anxiety he couldn't overcome. Now at home, every conversation with Celia was a path to the same topic: making a baby. A baby scared Zak, but not as much as Celia's urgency. She acted as if their suburban middle-class privileges would be revoked if they didn't soon produce an heir for their manicured lawn and unopened Tiki torches lost in the garage.

She turned off the television.

"What about the party?" she asked.

"What about it?"

Celia finished her wine. "The theme made me think of old times." She paused. Her voice was soft now and mindful, almost as if she knew how he spent his afternoons: face in front of the computer screen, trying to make himself work again. She left for the kitchen. Wine splashed into the glass. "I called Human Resources at Nationwide. There are a few positions I think you'd like."

He waited for her to say a second income is essential for the baby. Instead, she knocked in an uneven pattern on the wall from the kitchen. He moved to the wall to feel the vibrations. They used to be so in sync, so connected, so willing to corrupt each other's bodies, never losing the reason to explore their limits, and then at some point life's predictability eradicated their corruption.

He moved from the knocking to the dining room window. Outside, Colleen Kellerman—president of the Home Owners Association—traversed the sidewalk, clipboard in hand. Every month she threw a themed party—tomorrow's was heroes and villains. The last one was a murder mystery. Zak was the killer. Now, amongst the cul-de-sac, "Killer" became his nickname. Colleen stopped in front of the Burnishes. She took pictures of the Burnish's property with her phone and then scribbled on her clipboard. Probably writing a citation for things she deemed "Eyesores," which were requests to address an infraction of the cul-de-sac's bylaws—which updated every three months. People like Colleen were the reason Zak had fought Celia on moving to the suburbs. "We can't trust Columbus public schools," Celia said. The day after they moved in, Colleen visited. She introduced herself, gave them a gift basket, and then mentioned that their mailbox wasn't painted white, which was an issue because it marred the street's symmetry. That night, Celia rubbed her naked-self against him, but all he could see was Colleen's gift basket, and for the first time in his life, he realized it does happen to every guy.

"I'll remodel the kitchen," he said, knowing he couldn't. He closed one eye and pretended to squish Colleen's head with his fingers. "I'll watch Youtube videos and do the whole thing."

Celia appeared. "Why not start with the hole in the basement or that squeaky step. I'm ordering dinner. Thai sound good?" She headed back to the kitchen.

He ignored the placation in her voice and watched Colleen strut back to her house. He pressed his middle finger against the window and whispered, "Die."

And then it happened.

It moved.

A reflexive kick.

Like a leg in the womb.

@

Celia rubbed lotion on her thighs. Zak flipped through the television channels, craning his neck to look past her. He wondered if she'd get up in the morning to run. She'd regained that skinny, toned form she had when they first met, back when they'd have sex in public places because they couldn't wait until they got home to be that close to one another.

"We should go to the Kellermans' Party."

"'Hey, Killer.' Pass."

He turned off the television.

Silence.

In the city a horn blaring, a neighbor screaming, or sirens sirening challenged the silence, bringing conversation.

Now.

Just.

Silence.

"We're designated as super villains. I can go as Poison Ivy, and since you do such a good impression, you should go as the Joker."

Back when Zak was great at his sales job, he talked like Al Pacino and Christopher Walken and Jack Nicholson to explain what the drugs did. His clients loved it. But somewhere along the way, the more they asked for the voices, the less he did them until he stopped altogether.

"Good night," she said and squeezed his hand before slipping on her sleeping mask.

Zak lay awake. Would tonight be the night he'd awaken to her taking him into her mouth like she'd done many times before . . . perhaps too many times, until the nocturnal violation became too routine . . . too familiar . . . too polite.

The next morning Lance Reynolds arrived at ten-thirty with a satchel draped over his right shoulder and a portfolio tucked under his left arm. He made a comment about Zak still being in his robe, and then moved about the house, scrutinizing every room but the kitchen. At the top of the steps, Zak thought about pushing Lance, wondering if that pesky bottom step would squeak as he tumbled past it. This thought warmed him.

"I'll admit, when the Petersons sold this place, I was peeved they didn't contract me as their realtor. Old people? Am I right?"

Zak led him to the kitchen.

"I see what your wife is talking about. With this wall gone, the first floor would feel bigger. Open concept makes everything seem less restrictive." He nodded. "Yep. A great kitchen makes a house finally feel like home."

Lance took measurements and talked about pendant lights and how granite countertops would be a nice addition. "We can even put a burner and a sink in the island if you'd like. Updating a kitchen makes the house more livable and twice as nice to a prospective buyer if you ever choose to sell." Lance set the tape measure down and asked Zak if he had questions.

"Who's the redhead?" Zak said.

Lance looked at Zak as if he was finally interesting.

"You just cut right to it, don't you, Turner?"

"I hate small talk."

"I thought you were in sales."

"Transition period."

Lance looked at Zak's robe and nodded. "Belle's just something to do until Audrey gets back from Africa." His hesitation spawned a grin. "You know, Audrey actually told me to 'sow my wild oats' while she was gone. And you know what? I intend to sow every last one of them over and over and over until that ring is on my finger." He grinned. "She gets me. I said I'd never marry again, but Audrey," he shrugged. "Millennials are afraid to enforce morality as if being moral is a silent attack of judgment on someone somewhere. Whatever. To social liberation." He went back to work. "You probably have a support beam here. We could cover it with a pillar, but we wouldn't be able to totally open up the room."

"The whole neighborhood sees the redhead leave in the morning. Don't you care what people think?"

"If I'm happy, then how could I possibly care what Frances Burnish or Howard Havenshaw or Crazy Ginny Scuro thinks of me?"

"What about Colleen Kellerman?"

"You're like goddamn Jimmy Stewart at a window." He paused. "Get this: I'm taking Belle to Kellerman's party."

"Why?"

"Consider Belle more of a prop than a date." He laughed. "Belle's white southern trash appeal will throw off the social symmetry of Colleen's party. I can't wait. Besides, it'll be good for Colleen. She has to learn she can't control everything."

Lance put his yellow legal pad and measuring tape in his satchel. He handed over the portfolio. "I always find home improvement is easier if you steal an idea. In the meantime, I'll contact my people about initial estimates on the construction." He made a clicking sound. "Talk to you later, Killer."

Zak watched Lance walk home. Colleen darted out of her house and chased him down the sidewalk. Lance chomped at the sky, laughing at Colleen.

*The head of a puppet.*

She crossed her arms and tapped her foot as Lance kept walking. Then, with a quick peek in all directions, she hurried to his house, where the door was open.

Zak placed his hand in the hole in the basement wall. He did this often. He liked to remember the horrific wonder in Celia's eyes when he made it, and how creating it made him feel powerful. That night was the last time they'd had sex. She charged him, mocking his predictable maleness, and his need to punch something at rest. He threw her down and she laughed at him. She continued to laugh until her moans took over and her hands pushed him into her.

That was seven months ago.

"Zak? You down there?" Celia shouted.

Zak removed his hand from the hole and went upstairs. She handed him a "gift." Zak pulled the plastic bag over the hanger to reveal a purple, pinstriped suit. Celia opened a brown bag showing green tights, black shorts, a green bustier, and a red wig. Underneath was a face painting kit. He dug his bare toes into the light blue, shag carpet.

"What do you think?" Celia asked.

"I think you want me to dress up like a clown."

"The Joker *is* a clown." She pulled out her bustier. "And what about me? Poison Ivy is pretty sexy. Yes? Remember how it used to turn you on, watching me flirt with all other guys at a party, only to see their faces when I left with you?"

Zak held out the suit and shook his head. "New theme, same party."

Celia cradled the bag. She exhaled and widened her eyes. "I need this, Zak. Please." The bag crinkled and crunched at its compression. She wiped her eye with her shoulder. "At work, they call me B.W.P." She looked at Zak. "Bitch With Power."

Her open eyes released tears. Zak should've stroke her hair—that always calmed her—but he didn't because he didn't want to stop her pain. He moved closer, looming, but not touching.

"Please, please, please, let's forget who we are for a little while. Just a few hours." When Zak didn't respond, she mumbled a curse and went to the kitchen. Concealed by the wall she said, "Did Lance drop this off?" After the sound of flipping pages ceased, she was out the door.

There was a small gathering on Lance's lawn. Aside from the hair color, his wife and the redhead looked similar. Same height. Same skinny waist. Same full bosom. Same long, skinny legs. Same narrow hips. Celia was the first in her family to go to college. First in her family to do much of anything. Celia tried to erase her past, but when drunk, her small-town simplicity emerged. Zak loved that part of her, but with each passing year, it felt further and further away.

Celia shook the redhead's hand and then opened Lance's portfolio. Lance flashed a smile and then said something to make Celia laugh. The redhead laughed too and then stroked Lance's back as she stared at Celia. He imagined Celia grabbing their hands and leading them into Lance's house.

The warmness came back.

He grabbed the toolbox and moved to the base of the stairs. He yanked up the decorative runner covering the squeaking step and pounded in nail after nail. With each nail, he felt his underwear stretch.

He strolled to Lance's. His wife was at the end of the driveway talking to the redhead. He squeezed the hammer's handle as Lance gave his rose bush careful attention, trimming it. Lance pointed at Zak with the clippers. Zak pointed back with his hammer.

"I'm the only person in the cul-de-sac that does his own land-scaping. Everyone else—you included—uses that Ulysses guy that Colleen commands. You know what my lawn offers? Originality and pride."

Zak brandished the hammer.

"You like my wife?"

Lance shrugged. "Is that not allowed?"

Zak scanned the cul-de-sac. Everything seemed different from this angle. The redhead laughed at something his wife said.

"Looks like the ladies are getting along."

Zak knocked the hammer against the stucco. Lance stood.

"Belle has a kid—which is usually a deal breaker for me—but it's the best sex I've ever had. I mean ever. The things this woman will do to please me. It's like my subconscious coming to life."

Zak hit the stucco harder.

"Anyway, gotta end it with Belle after the party tonight. She's getting too attached." Lance knelt and picked off dead leaves from a rose bush. "Belle's biologically necessary though. After Audrey and I get hitched, I'll need those crazy sex memories to hold me over until death do us part." Lanced laughed. "Jesus. I don't know if I'll ever meet Belle's sexual ambition again. It's downright reckless."

"Tell me about Colleen."

Zak tried to knock the hammer against the stucco again, but Lance grabbed his wrist. Zak imagined plunging the reverse end into Lance's forehead. That warmness came back. Lance's grip tightened. Zak grew warmer.

"I'm gonna replace that stucco, just not today."

Zak lowered the hammer. "Colleen."

Lance looked at the women. "Here's what I've learned. Every woman wants the right guy to make her feel safe enough to be dirty. They call them rape fantasies or some shit. I don't know. I just know I'm good at creating that moment for them. And once you figure out the fucked up, twisted hidden desire they want you to exploit, I promise you this: you can't go back. This is why love is dangerous. It's too safe."

Once Zak surprised Celia at night in her office building. He snuck up behind her while she was walking a dimly lit corridor and grabbed her from behind. She struggled at first, maybe not knowing it was him, maybe never even realizing, but she still reached for his zipper, and without looking back, bent over a desk, uniting them in selfish perversion. It was the closest he'd ever felt to anyone.

@

Neither talked as they prepared for the party. Celia stopped applying her make-up and looked at him.

"Tonight should be fun. Like old times. I need an old-timesy kinda of a night."

On the day he quit, Zak stopped at the automatic sliding doors to the hospital. Open. Close. Open. Close. He shook his satchel and listened to the pills shake. A woman in a wheelchair holding a baby exited. The man by her side looked at Zak. His face was overwhelmed with fear. He opened a car door and said something about not knowing how the car seat worked. The woman handed him the baby and said, "Neither do I." The man held the baby out, away from him, aimed at Zak, as if it were a fragile relic he should not be trusted with. Zak turned back to the doors. Open. Close. Open. Close. He knew if he walked through them—as expected— one day he'd exit them just like that couple.

He removed the purple blazer. "I'm not going."

Celia looked at him in the mirror. His throat expanded as he swallowed. She moved her eyes to the faucet, keeping them wide as she breathed out her nose.

"Shocker," she said, pulling up her green tights.

Zak went to the basement. He put his hand in the hole. Out. In. Out. In. Out. In. He found a sledgehammer behind the water heater. He'd never seen it before. Its head was nothing more than a scarred, lopsided mass of metal.

After Celia left, he went to the kitchen and faced the wall. After a few swings, plaster crunched beneath his feet as he danced from the kitchen to the living room.

The warmness started.

Looking in Celia's vanity, he applied the make-up from the kit. First, his face went white, then he outlined his eyes with black, then he did crude smearing of red over his lips, curling his smile halfway up his cheek. He rubbed his brown hair green and greased it back.

A stranger appeared.

The warmness grew hot.

Music emanated from the Kellermans. He skulked to the dining room window, gripping the sledgehammer. Inside, heroes and villains mingled with blood red cocktails in their hands. Celia was laughing. The Poison Ivy outfit expounded her breasts and her green tights hugged her long legs. Lance Reynolds, dressed as Superman, palmed the redhead's Wonder Woman's skirt. Zak gripped the hammer's handle and moved to Colleen's mailbox. His second target was Lance's stucco.

Back inside, he positioned himself in a pocket of darkness. The anticipation made him feel lucid and morally invincible.

She screamed his name when she saw the hole in the wall. He squeezed the sledgehammer's handle. She stepped through the wall and screamed his name again. Her anger infiltrated him, erecting goosebumps. She stared his way, curious. He thrust his glowing face from the darkness, raising the sledgehammer, cuing her scream.

Fear made her movements clumsy. She fell between scattered sheetrock. He hovered over her as she lay within the wall. Her fists beat his heaving chest and the fire in his stomach spread to his loins. He tossed the sledgehammer and pulled her underneath him. His painted face laughed silently. The more she squirmed, the stiffer he became. He held both her wrists with one hand and groped her with the other, stretching out his neck, as if to merge his face with the paint. He looked up at the opening he'd created and moved against her with forceful familiarity, and as his rhythm steadied, she clenched a piece of drywall with wanton understanding, squeezing it, until it burst.

# Rose

HER MOTHER PARKED their dirty green sedan on the wrong side of the street—the one that had moved them from Alabama, to South Carolina, to Georgia, to Tennessee, to Kentucky, and now to Ohio. Rose looked in the cracked passenger mirror, to the road leading out of the cul-de-sac, away from Lance Reynolds' pristine landscaping, to someplace broken and more familiar.

"If I had a gun, I'd drive away," her mother sang.

There was something hateful in the lyrics and Rose couldn't bear to listen to her mother's voice blend perfectly with Diana Jones' sullen pitch. Belle, her mother, couldn't carry a tune, not even "Happy Birthday," but when it came to Jones' haunting ballad, Belle's voice was right on key.

Rose looked at the "For Sale" sign next to a naked flagpole in the yard beside their car. "What's the plan, Mama? Lance'll learn to love ya if we move to his street?" Rose cringed, her southern drawl more prominent than her sarcasm. She bit the tip of a fingernail. Behind the flagpole, a cardinal landed on a gutter. In school, she'd learned that some birds mate for life: turtle doves, bald eagles, swans, penguins, and albatrosses. Cardinals didn't make that list. Neither did humans. Wolves did though. So did beavers. But not humans. From what Rose could tell, humans meet the one love of their life, and then, after they lose that love, they force its existence in others. Rose balanced an acrylic nail chip on her tongue. The cardinal flew away. She rolled down the window and spat out the nail.

"Lily-bear, don't do that. It's not womanly." Belle grabbed Rose's chin. "You're a mess, girl. Got lipstick on your teeth. Watch." Belle rubbed her index finger across her bleached enamel. "Like that. Now, you go." Rose thought about rolling her top lip down to smear red over her teeth but followed orders.

"In Alabama," her mother continued, "back when I was a Little Miss Crimson, I'd rub Vaseline on my teeth to ensure smiling. Tulip, sometimes I think that's what you need. Something a little extra to ensure that smile."

"You put something toxic in your mouth on purpose?"

"It's not toxic, Tulip. The guy who invented it ate a tablespoon every morning."

"Listening to the inventor of crazy doesn't make it less crazy, mom," Rose said in her best northern accent.

Belle gave Rose a concerned look. "Good looks will get you farther than your smart mouth, girl. A guy will do darn near anything for a beautiful woman." Rose shook her head and looked away. Belle pushed Rose's hair behind her left ear. "Now, don't you fret, Lily-bear, your womanly qualities will sprout soon. You're just a late bloomer is all." She winked. "Your form will trigger criminal thoughts soon enough."

At thirteen, Rose had yet to get her period. She had lied to her classmates about it so she wouldn't be teased. She tried to lie to her mother too, but Belle saw right through her. This was around the time Belle began checking Rose's chest every morning for "breast buds." Rose had no use for a bra; her chest looked the same as it did when she was six. Belle said when Rose's breasts finally sprout, one would no doubt be bigger than the other, but soon she'd rely on them, making them a part of her personality, maybe even name them. Her mother then fondled her C cups and said, "Like Thelma and Louise here." Moments like that made Rose practice her northern accent. Her dad was from the north, a small town in Pennsylvania. When she sped up her vowels and picked up the pace of her speech, she thought—from what she could remember—that she sounded like him.

Using the visor mirror, Belle re-applied lipstick. She pursed her full lips together like she often did when she knew she looked beautiful. "You get your lack of development from your daddy's side," Belle said. "Your Aunt Maggie was eleven years older than your daddy and flat as a board with wide birthing hips. Poor thing looked like an upside down opened umbrella. Come to think of it, your daddy was raised by flat chests. He must've took one look at these babies, and that was it: hook, line, and sinker." She flipped up the visor. "But you got your legs from your Mama's side. Your stride is gonna serve you just fine." She smiled at Rose. "You think I'm wrong about all this, but you'll see soon enough. All that matters to men is hot lookin' and good cookin'." Belle skipped back three songs and cued up Diana Jones again. Rose stared at the glove compartment, wondering if she'd find a loaded gun there. Wouldn't have been the first time.

She focused on the eyelashes. How silly to feel them. Before leaving, Belle applied a heavy coat of mascara on her. Rose stared in the mirror as Belle used black eyeliner to hollow out Rose's blue eyes, giving them the icy look she so often saw in her mother. She hated wearing make-up, but once she started middle school, her mother painted her up to camouflage her stunted development. "You don't want teased, but you don't want un-noticed neither."

Rose tried not to think about the gunk on her face and looked at the pruned hedges in front of Lance's house. Tulips and lilies were budding. Ivy climbed up the front side of the house. She thought it looked like a home out of a magazine, making it not feel real.

"Can't we just go, Mama? Lance probably has some new girl by now. Guys like him always do." The rising sun shot through the windshield making Rose squint. In science class, Rose had learned that the streams of light jutting off the sun were an illusion. It made her think of all the pictures she'd drawn when she was younger—pictures of herself and her mother and the spectacular sun's rays shining down on them.

Belle's hands tightened over the steering wheel as she sang Jones' chorus. "A new girl? Who's to say?" Belle said, with a haughty, indignant pitch that made Rose tap her foot. The last time Belle spoke like this was back in Tennessee right before she threw a rock through the windshield of Earl Esch's truck.

Afterward, Belle's glasslike eyes stared at Rose as she justified heaving the rock, saying it was a magnanimous act, protecting all parties involved, especially Earl's wife. Rose stared at the shards of glass on the asphalt and wanted to cut herself, to help her mother understand pain.

"Mom, let's just go home. Remember Tennessee?"

After the Earl incident, Rose spent three weeks in foster care. She still had vivid nightmares about those weeks. Fed once a day—at four in the afternoon—always macaroni and cheese. She counted the stains on the ceiling to keep her mind occupied. An older boy slept in the same room. He'd asked Rose to watch him masturbate. Said he wouldn't touch her, but he'd like her to watch was all. She suffered the stench of the blanket as she kept it over her face, trying to block out his grunts.

"Earl did wrong, Buttercup. Not me. He needed to learn his lesson. That's all."

"Whatever."

Despite shunning his marital vows, Rose liked Earl. He never had a kid of his own and was good to her. He was sad and lonely. She trusted his pain.

Cars left the cul-de-sac. The residents of Vintage Woods Court waved as they passed. Rose waved back. What would life be like if courtesy was always common?

"Mom," she said, after another person waved, "tell me a Dad story." Belle smiled and grabbed Rose's hand. Rose liked her mother's hands. They were soft and little.

"Your father had the most perfect teeth. He didn't need braces and they always stayed so white. Best smile I'd ever seen." Something light and cheerful was now playing. Rose didn't recognize it. "All the girls were so jealous of me when they'd see your father holding my hand. My whole life I was told I was pretty, but I never truly felt pretty until I met your father."

An ache attacked her stomach. What if that white truck hadn't started that morning? What if her dad missed a green light? What if the driver of the white truck didn't spill coffee on his lap?

"Get down, Tulip!"

Rose sank in the seat, her dress riding up her back. A car zoomed by. When they sat up, the car that had been in Lance's driveway was gone.

"Tulip, baby, what we are doing ain't wrong. Just a little research to make sure Lance ain't no liar." She looked in the visor mirror and checked her face. "All we're doing's investigating a rumor. I want to be wrong. I really do. Because if I'm wrong, I can trust men again."

"Lance sucked, Mom. He isn't worth this—whatever it is. Let's go home." She raised her voice an octave to sound optimistic. "You can work on a new recipe." Belle's cookbook had received rejection after rejection. Rose compiled the recipes. She charted the ingredients, the measurements, and the directions because her mother could never remember what she did as she cooked. Belle said cooking was "emotional improvisation" and that the ingredients spoke to her, telling her what to do. And even though Rose thought she was accurate, Belle could never recreate the same tasting meal based on her notes.

"Cooking's all we need, Mom," she said after a silence, thinking about how no man had watched her mother cook. "Cooking's all we need."

Belle closed her eyes and grabbed Rose's hands. "May the gods of trust grant you passage to all things honest and decent in this world so you can carry that innocence forever." Rose hated when her mother spoke like some preacher. Belle grew up in a small town overrun with extreme Baptists. Rose visited once and everyone talked like they were reading scripture, delivering judgment.

"Now if something happens," her mother continued, "and law officials misinterpret the situation, it's best to look like a lady, hear? So, let's get our story straight. We are from the Evangelical Holy Temple of Deliverance and we are there to pick up Lance's most blessed donations for our congregation." Belle laughed, a small emission at first, then it grew louder and louder. Rose pursed her lips and clenched her fists. Belle pulled out nametags with EVANGELICAL HOLY TEMPLE OF DELIVERANCE printed in bold underneath their phony names. Rose was Charlotte and

Belle was Scarlett. "We'll be sisters this time." Her mom winked and clasped the pin to Rose's dress.

"Twins?"

"Don't be silly. I'm obviously younger."

Walking to Lance's front door, Rose tried to straighten her nametag, but it kept dipping to one side. Belle pushed a key into the lock until it clicked. "Where did you get that key?" Her mother didn't answer, just disappeared into the darkened foyer. Rose stayed on the front stoop, her sundress sticking to her back. Her mother called in a lyrical voice, and Rose followed her mother's song.

The one time Rose had been here, Lance didn't know what to do with her, like he'd never been around a kid before. Belle shooed them out of the kitchen so she could make homemade Humming Bird Cake. Lance pressed his index finger against his lips and motioned for Rose to follow him up the stairs. His bedroom looked like something out of a catalog—from a store her mother couldn't afford—with velvet throw pillows and a cherry headboard. "Have a seat on the bed," he said before entering the closet. Her throat itched, sitting on the very bed where her mother and Lance did it. Lance returned with a small wooden chest. He sat next to Rose and motioned to open it. Inside was an assortment of jewelry. "Take whatever you want," he said and left the room. She pushed aside bracelets and rings and earrings. A lot of the earrings didn't have a match. A silver necklace with a silver rose pendant attached caught her eye. She unclasped it and held it to her neckline in front of the mirror. It was pretty. But she was afraid her mother wouldn't let her keep it, afraid she'd be jealous that she had been alone with Lance, so rather than put it on, she slid it into her pocket. Walking up the stairs, she wondered: Had her mom added to the little chest? A trinket lost amid the rest of Lance's conquests?

She followed Belle into Lance's bedroom. Belle sifted through receipts pulled from an open drawer. Rose balled up her hands and leaned against the wall. She'd seen *Law and Order: SVU*: leave no fingerprints. Belle brandished the receipts. "The Florentine? Barrel 44? The Elevator? I've never even heard of these restaurants. 'I love your cooking. No restaurant cooks barbecue like you, Belle.' Buttercup, you're thirteen years old, 'bout time you learn that love ain't no more than a well-dressed lie." She opened a drawer and pulled out folded t-shirts and threw them on the floor. "Have you ever seen a man so put together?" She emptied the drawers, and then unmade the bed and threw the pillows against the wall. Rose shut her eyes. Not even the sound of the lamp hitting the wall made her open them.

The first time Rose met Lance, her mother had prepared a big southern dinner at their apartment. She'd made all the fixin's: fried chicken, collard greens, corn bread, black-eyed peas, sweet potato casserole, and a pecan pie for dessert. She had even sprung for a bottle of Beringer Merlot to impress him. After he left, while they cleaned the dishes, Rose said, "Lance is bad news. He likes himself too much. Guys like him don't change." Belle smiled as she scrubbed the grease stuck to the pan. "We'll see," she said, before humming something beautiful.

Belle yanked Rose away from the wall and marched out of the room. "It'd be a box about this big." She made a small square with her hands. "Open your eyes!" Rose stood before a custom-made bookshelf in the loft. Her mother pointed to it. "You know the kind of box I mean, right? Go on, now."

Belle went downstairs. Rose moved away from the book-shelf and poked her head through wrought iron spindles, her hands grasping two bars. The room below looked like a painting. Everything was in place. Nothing on the floor. No indention in the couch. The carpet had fresh vacuum tracks.

A drawer ripped open. Silverware clashed against itself. Pots hit the floor. Rose held onto the bars and leaned back, looking up at the cathedral ceilings that made the great room below feel so big. When she was older, she'd live in a studio apartment, just one big open room, with no inner walls.

Rose picked up a phone on the bookshelf, but there was no dial tone. She wiped down the phone with the base of her dress. Her mom's truculence reverberated, bouncing off the high ceiling, down to her. When Lance came, home, he'd know they'd been there. She un-balled her fists.

"I'm going back through his bedroom again." Belle climbed the steps. "Check the office." When she reached the top of the stairs Rose wanted to push her mother backward so she'd break a leg. Then Rose would stuff her in a closet so when Lance came home, she could overhear him commenting on her craziness.

"Rose. The office! Now!"

Being called by her name surprised her. She didn't move until her mother patted her bottom and said, "Scoot."

A handmade oak executive desk sat in the middle of the room. Rose sank into the leather chair and faced the doorway. She imagined Lance sitting in the chair, talking real estate business or something; she couldn't even pretend what adults talked about. The leather stuck to the back of her thighs as she swiveled. Rose remembered her dad leaving for work, but Belle had never said what he did for a living, just that he was important, a big-to-do, a somebody.

A picture of Lance with a red-headed woman sat on the desk. She looked a lot like Belle, but younger. Rose ran her hand over the glass. She'd seen Lance smile before, but here, his eyes were lighter, more open, bluer. The last time Rose had seen Lance, she was outside, reading *Swallowing Stones* under a tree at the apartment complex. Lance seemed startled to see her. He said he had an open house and had to get going. Then he paused and looked right at her and said, "Good-bye, Rose" with such finality. She waved as Lance drove away, his SUV blending into the order of traffic along Hilliard-Rome Road.

Rose found a yellow highlighter in the middle desk drawer. She unclasped the frame and took out the picture of Lance and the redhead. On the opposite side, she drew a sun with as many rays as she could fit around the cartoon orb. She lined her sun against the glass and struggled to re-clasp the frame, pressing down so hard the glass split. A jagged edge cut her. She sucked on her index finger and set the frame where she'd found it.

Rose pressed her finger against her dress as she followed a banging noise to the kitchen. A metal lock box lay open on the kitchen floor. A hammer rested against it. Beside the hammer lay an empty leather ring box. Her mother was shaking. She held out her left hand and modeled a big sparkling diamond. The band pinched her skin.

"It's not round," Rose said. "I thought diamonds were round."

"It's a princess cut, Tulip. She must be his little princess." She stared at the diamond in disbelief. "Son-uv-a-bitch was telling the truth. 'I have a fiancée in Africa. Bought her a ring and everything. I'm keeping her ring here. She didn't want to show off such extravagance in such a poor place. You gotta believe me, Belle. She told me to have my fun, but be a one-woman man when she returned.'" She looked at Rose. "Why would I believe that story? What woman would actually say that? 'Have your fun?'"

"You didn't want him anyway, Mom. He wasn't a good one. Not like Dad."

Belle smiled at Rose, a smile that almost made Rose forget where they were. "Rosey, my problem is I met your daddy first."

"I love you, Mom," Rose said, not even embarrassed by the desperation in her voice. "Let's just go. Please. Let's just go."

"I know you love me." Belle smiled, her face burned red as she yanked at the ring. "I just wish that were enough." She pulled the ring off. A sadness overcame Belle's face, her eyes lucid, the opposite of their glassy, cold glaze after the incident with Earl's truck. A sunbeam blazed through the skylight. Rose watched as Belle held the ring to the light. A sly, duplicitous smile won over her mother's face.

"Buttercup, look! It's a fake. This is a fake diamond. It's not real. Look!" She thrust the ring in Rose's face, but it sparkled the same as it had a few minutes ago. "This ring is a lie."

The force of the hammer rattled the dishes in the cabinet. Rose expected to see glittered dust, something fantastical, but it simply shattered, as if glass dropped on concrete. "See. Fake." Her mother winked with a composure that almost tricked Rose into thinking everything would be okay.

Back home, Rose stared at a stain on the couch while spinning her fake nametag on the coffee table. Belle sang in the kitchen. She was making a surprise for Rose, a new dish. This wouldn't go in the cookbook; it was just for her. Rose looked at her finger where the picture frame had cut it. She picked up the nametag and unclasped the pin. She stuck her finger, drawing a spot of blood. It hurt. She didn't know why she did it, yet, she felt like doing it to another finger, so she did. After she pricked all the fingers on her left hand she went to the kitchen and watched her mother dice tomatoes. Belle was so careful with her cooking, so methodical and so free at the same time. It reminded her of the way Mrs. Meyer, her English teacher, had described poetry: *words waiting for you to discover humanity.*

"Ten minutes, Tulip. Go on. Get washed up," her mother said, as she mixed powdered sugar into the bubbling butter in the skillet. Rose tossed the nametag in the trash and headed for the bathroom.

After Rose washed the blood from her left hand, she looked at herself in the mirror. She missed her face. The gunk's gotta go. She sat on the edge of the tub and pinched the tiny holes in her fingers while waiting for the shower to warm. After the mirror had fogged up, she removed her clothes. This was a habit she had formed so she wouldn't have to see her naked reflection. She opened a drawer and took the rose pendant out of a Dove box. She'd never worn it, afraid her mother would see her as competition. In the back of the drawer, under an unopened box of Stay Free pads, were blades she'd removed from her disposable razors. It took so long to remove each blade, she felt it a waste to throw them away. Shadowed feet settled on the other side of the door. "Lilly-bear, you okay? Why are you showering?" Rose covered her mouth, her hand hitting her teeth, the razor blade pinched between her fingers, inches from her eye. "Dinner's ready in five minutes." The footsteps disappeared. She cleared a spot on the mirror with a couple of swipes. She held the razor between her index finger and her thumb and lightly dragged it across her stomach. Watching herself wince, Rose admired her teeth: so white and so straight. She threaded the necklace's chain through the hole in the razor until it pushed against the rose pendant. She fastened the necklace, feeling the charms sway against her chest, as she stepped into the shower.

# Signs

COLLEEN KELLERMAN NODDED when her stylist asked if she was sure she wanted to cut off all her hair. "And get rid of the black-dye job while you're at it." Watching her hair fall, she thought of Phil, her estranged husband. Phil had a thing for *exotic* women—Asian and South American—or at least that's what his Internet search history suggested. So, a few years ago, Colleen grew her hair out and stained it dark. To her surprise, Phil took a liking to it, which resurrected their sex-life, which resolved her inner-debate: she no longer loved him. But still, she didn't want him to leave. Divorce was so public. So incongruous. So . . .

"It's called Resting Bitch Face," the twenty-something next to her said, pointing at Colleen in the mirror. "I have it too." She tapped her wrinkle-free face.

"I'm sorry?" Colleen said.

"RBF."

"RBF?"

"Resting Bitch Face. You know, when you're just mindlessly sitting there, thinking about something dumb, like a song from high school, then people see your face—your normal face—and just assume you're a bitch."

"That's not a thing," Colleen said.

"Oh, it's a thing. Scientists have confirmed it. Even has its own Wikipedia page."

Her stylist nodded. "It's half the reason people come in. They want something to offset it."

"Offset their face?" Colleen said.

"Exactly," the twenty-something said. "I'm going to a wedding this weekend. What do single people do at a wedding? Recruit. I want them to look at my hair, my legs, my tits: not my face." She ran her hands through her hair. "Speaking of: cut it short, but nothing pretentious. Nothing that says I'm trying too hard to be trusted—I'm not reading the six-o-clock news." She shrugged. "Something fun. And cute. Sophomore year of college cute. God, that was a good year." She swiped at her phone. "I'll find you a picture."

Inches and inches of dark hair fell to the floor.

"So, why the change?" the stylist asked Colleen.

After Phil left, she went skydiving. She wanted to update her Facebook profile picture with a shot of her freefalling through the clouds to anger Phil since skydiving was something he always wanted to do. When the first parachute didn't open, she assumed it was the end. After passing through a cloud, her mind moved to her son Jimmy, the beautiful, artistic boy she didn't understand. She spread out her arms, embracing the fall, wondering if her death would make his poetry better. Then the contingency chute opened.

"I'm running for School Board," Colleen said. "Consider this my campaign cut."

"Good luck with that," the twenty-something said. "I taught high school for one year. Now I'm a pharmaceutical sales rep." She rolled her eyes as she looked at her phone. "A daily coffee enema is more alluring than one minute back in public education."

"I just want to help my . . ." she trailed off. "Oh my God." She leaned closer to the mirror. "Oh my God." Her brows angled down, advertising a promised shrewdness in her hazel eyes. This—mixed with her prominent cheekbones and lineless forehead—gave the permanent impression she was plotting something horrific. After deeming her face objectively confrontational, she said, "I could strike fear in every Disney princess."

The twenty-something winked. "Welcome to the club."

@

Colleen listened to her self-help CD on her way to Kinkos. It was about the fear of being judged and had played on a loop since Phil left. All it did was make her think of Lance, her neighbor.

Two years ago at her Christmas movie themed holiday party, Lance pointed at a picture of her when she was in her twenties. "Look at you," he said, wearing that pink bunny costume from *A Christmas Story*. "I mean, look at you." She told him it was before Jimmy. Before Phil. Before this life. "What were you? A hiccup out of college?" She said it was the summer after. "I like your hair that color," he grinned. "Like the sun."

When she pulled into the parking lot, Jimmy was hunched over his Moleskine notebook. She never asked him what he wrote because she was certain she wouldn't understand it. She wasn't dumb—quite the opposite—however, she considered herself only corporate America intelligent. When it came to truths of emotion and human sensibilities, she might as well have been a toddler trying to recall the intricacies of her first nightmare. But Jimmy read Byron and Keats and Donne at the dinner table. She marveled how the DNA of her emotional detachment and Phil's unapologetic love for all things dude had created an old soul who watched TMC, did crosswords, and listened to Bach.

Jimmy looked up at the click of her heels. Colleen planted a hand on a hip and posed. "You're right. Dad's leaving isn't getting to you at all."

Inside, the campaign signs sat at the checkout. She held one up for Jimmy. The border was in blue, the words in white, and the background in red. She pushed her face to the glossy sheen searching for a reflection.

"You know I'm graduating next year," Jimmy said.

"I'm a whole person outside of being your mother," she said, putting the sign down, having no idea what she meant.

Bobby, Kinkos' ace employee, returned from the back, reeking of pot. "Whoa. Citizen's arrest, lady. That sign's not yours."

"Bobby," Colleen said, "it's me."

The way Bobby smiled—embarrassed that he didn't recognize her, yet, not ashamed of the perversion dancing in his eyes—made her think of Lance.

"Wow. Mrs. K., I didn't recognize you. You look . . . I mean the blonde," Bobby grinned, "It's hot. Really hot. And not just for an older lady. You look hot for, like, any lady." Without taking his eyes off her, he said, "What's up, Jimbo?"

Colleen ignored her son's desperate plea of "dude."

"Aren't you sweet, Bobby," Colleen said, scouring for a reflective façade. *Seriously, an entire store built around producing replicas and facsimiles and not one surface to cast a reflection.* Her mother taught her life is less painful if she found its irony. After Phil said he was leaving her for good, he marched up to their bedroom and took a nap.

After shutting the Traverse's back door, Bobby lingered in front of the driver side window. He'd probably have sex with her right then if she'd let him. She entertained this thought, but noted red flags: they'd have to move the signs, her son stood two feet away, and then there was the daunting task of directing Bobby on how to satisfy her. The prospect of that annoyance murdered the imaginative tryst. She'd never had an orgasm with Phil, or with anyone before Phil for that matter. Not even alone. She found masturbation to be a silly, solipsistic pursuit. If she was going to do something for herself that took physical effort and precision, she might as well vacuum the house.

She studied her reflection in the rearview mirror. Under the short blonde hair appeared the same eyes, the same resting face. "Fear of judgment is a future stopper. No action can transpire if judgment is your only audience." She closed her eyes and rhythmically breathed in and out ten times before opening them. When she opened her eyes, Bobby gave a crooked look, full of anticipatory guilt, like he'd just walked in on his mother showering, but chose not to leave right away.

"Hope you, uh, win, Mrs. Kellerman," Bobby said. Jimmy hugged Bobby and whispered something in his ear. Bobby winked and said, "gimme a day."

Colleen suddenly needed Jimmy to ride home with her. "Load up your bike."

"There's no room." When she didn't react, he shook his head and pointed. "The campaign signs." It took a few seconds to realize what he was talking about.

@

Colleen pushed a sign in the Longstreth's yard. Each house in the *Peephole* advertised their support. She'd invented the playful sobriquet after identifying Vintage Woods Court making her descent to Columbus International Airport from Midway. From the heavens, their cul-de-sac looked just like an old-fashioned keyhole. Being the president and founder of the HOA for their cul-de-sac, Colleen deemed things "Eyesores," and issued citations, marking which HOA code was in breach. Coordinating mailbox color was a collective pleasantry. Repainting shutters and doors enriched the street's aesthetic vibe. She thought it was a fun, silly thing to do, although no one seemed to understand its joke. This led to residential placation in promoting her as an authority figure who maintained the street's visual harmony, earning her the nickname, Frau Kellerman.

She glared at Lance Reynolds' house. He'd given Colleen her first orgasm on her fortieth birthday. Every time she thought of him, that piece of personal trivia became intertwined with her current thought. She grimaced. Lance's tulip bulbs were sprouting with spatial chaos. Would Lance ever acquiesce and use her gardener? He was the only one on the cul-de-sac who didn't. At the end of his mulch bed, there was a budding red tulip. She thought of his penis. She wished she was holding it, caressing it, treating it like a joystick, shifting it as if it were a programmed toggle, making him pick up the phone to call her goddamn gardener.

Colleen aimed her middle finger at Lance's house. When she turned, Don Longstreth was at his window. Don had never strung a sentence together she felt was worth listening to, but now, since Don's wife had left him too and since their kids hung out all of the time, she felt like saying hi. She waved. He lowered his blinds.

@

Colleen sipped merlot while waiting for Jimmy. Because he was "governed by the moment," he was never on time. "No discipline in that boy," Phil would say. Phil played football at Ohio State and used his local celebrity to profit as a sports equipment salesman. He never understood his son who wouldn't "play catch" or "shoot hoops" or watch "the game." Jimmy further wedged the divide by talking about poetry and books and history and philosophy just to embarrass his father, never seeing the irony in becoming his father's bully. Colleen intervened by working late, earning promotion after promotion.

A bottle of Merlot and a dinner courier later, she was still alone. She thought her shrimp scampi was too beautiful to eat, so she arranged it on the table as if it were plastic, and she lived in a show house. It'd grown dark, her blonde reflection prominent in the window. After a forced smile, she said, "Do I have your vote?"

In bed, she scrolled through Lance's texting history. Shots of him. Shots of her. His last message had been sent twenty-three days ago. "Sorry. No can do. She's back." She forgot all about Jimmy and her campaign and tried to put herself in a moment with Lance, something happy, but when she closed her eyes, all she could see was Don Longstreth closing his blinds.

@

Colleen took her morning coffee to the window. She wanted to enjoy her Starbuck's Hazelnut while looking at her signs.

"The hell?"

After a combination of quick, violent knocks, Don Longsteth answered. Colleen smiled as she smoothed down her robe.

"Good morning, Don."

"Got a problem with the color of my gutters?" he said, as he slipped a satchel over his tan jacket, locking the door behind him.

"Don, I know friends shouldn't talk politics—"

"We're friends?"

Not knowing how to circumvent that claim, she laughed.

He put his things in the car.

"The last time you talked to me, you told me that my shutters were fading and out of respect for the 'Peephole,' I should, and I quote, 'Get on top of that.'" Colleen absorbed his stare. He had soft brown, malleable eyes, like something she could scoop up with her finger and paint the walls. "You said that to me two days after Kelly left. Two days."

Colleen looked at his dark, forest green shutters and smiled.

"What do you want, Colleen? I have an early meeting with a parent."

Don was a guidance counselor at the high school, an ally, a voice from the inside. She took a deep breath. "Why did you remove my school board campaign sign from your lawn? I mean, if you don't want me on school board—"

"Colleen, *I* don't care if you're on the school board." Don pointed around the neighborhood. "But somebody does."

She spun, her adrenaline spike incited panic.

Every.

Sign.

Fucking.

Gone.

Just then, Lance Reynolds opened his front door and walked his fiancée to her car.

*What was her name?*

"Your face looks like you're posing for one of those turn of the century cameras that took thirty seconds to process," Don said.

"Sorry to have bothered you."

As she crossed the street, something guttural built inside her, a chaotic, scathing scream, like the one she felt when Phil said he was leaving, and just like then, she kept it inside.

Colleen paced behind Jimmy as he ate his cereal. Maybe Phil did it. It was something he'd do and then label it flirting. For Phil, romance and stupidity had become synonymous over the years, and he probably thought theft was a fetching game-changer in hopes to rekindle.

"We've been robbed!"

"What?" Jimmy carried his bowl to the sink.

"My signs. My campaign signs."

She closed her eyes, placed her chin on her chest, and breathed through her nose: *Judgment cannot be controlled, but only you can administer it power.*

"Mom, you're being a little dramatic, don't you think?"

"I try and try and try to make things nice, but people just seem to hate me."

"Trust is a lie to help us come undone—to follow winnings yet to become won."

She snapped her fingers. "I'm not your father. Don't speak to me in verse."

"Sorry. Geeze."

Jimmy walked across the street. Nikki Longstreth drove him to school. Jimmy kept refusing to get his license. He said it would force responsibility on him that wouldn't be true to his character. She gave them both the finger as they drove away.

She canceled her morning meeting and scribbled reasons not to start drinking. Feeling accomplished, she poured a glass of merlot. With glass number two came a familiar playful knock at the door. She looked in the mirror, running her hands through her blonde hair, and rubbing her face as if to restructure it.

"Come on, Colleen. I know you're home." Lance knocked. "We need to talk. It's about Junior."

She opened the door. Lance flashed his expensive smile, showing his white veneers, the ones she'd recommended so he'd look better in real estate advertisements.

"Whoa, Mama! Holy time warp. What have you done to yourself?" He reached for her hair, but she smacked his hand away.

"My son wants to be called Jimmy. So, call him Jimmy."

"Phil Jr.? Junior? Jimmy? Who cares. Look at you. Seriously, Colleen. I mean, how am I supposed to keep my promise now?" Lance smiled as if she was all that mattered in this world. She hated how he could give that look without consideration of consequence. She stared at a vase she didn't remember buying and fumbled with its plastic flowers. "You said this was about Jimmy."

They walked across the street, past the Longstreth's, beyond the open field, into the woods, towards the train tracks. As they ducked under the brush entering the tall evergreen trees, she grew optimistic. Maybe Lance's fiancée had found out about them and he was taking her to see *what's-her-names'* rotting corpse.

"There," Lance said, pointing to a mound of dead leaves. She looked back at Lance. He made a sweeping motion with his hand. She kicked the mound. Her campaign signs lay beneath.

"Why would you do this?"

"Not me. Phil Jr." Lance grabbed a sign, picked out the leaves in the wire, and stuck it in the ground. He shrugged. "I thought you should know. As a friend."

*Friend.* The word made her grind her teeth.

"What makes you think Jimmy did this?"

"I saw him."

"You saw him?"

Lance nodded.

She sat on a stump. Before it, large footprints were stamped in the dirt. Junior's feet. She looked at Lance and wanted to choke him, to stuff him in the mound of leaves with her signs. Instead, she walked over and kissed him hard. He moved his hands on her body, to her hair, then he pulled away. "Friends . . . remember?" She pulled her robe tight, reburied the signs, and endured a silent walk back to the Peephole.

Susan Tambourne waved Colleen over to her booth. Colleen asked who bleached Susan's teeth. Susan said she liked Colleen's new look and asked which salon was practicing sorcery these days. After the pleasantries, the two women grew silent. Susan cut the Panera cranberry muffin into four parts.

"I'm glad you called," Susan said. "I was worried our political rivalry would keep us from doing this—getting together. Politics and religion, am I right?" Susan smiled and pointed to the cranberry muffin. Colleen complied, and then ate another piece.

"I called," Colleen said, wiping her mouth, "because I don't want this election to come between us. Friendship is important."

Susan reached for Colleen's hands. "I know a big reason for running is to get creative writing back into the high school curriculum. I'm all for that too. From what I hear, your boy is quite the writer. I'm assuming you're going to the school's poetry slam this evening."

"Of course," Colleen said, not knowing what that meant.

"My daughter gets headaches reading billboards, but she's going to a poetry event because Junior is hosting. She has such a crush on him. I told her to get in line. I'm sure Junior has to beat them off with a stick!"

Colleen took another muffin bite. "Susan, have you ever heard of resting bitch face?"

Susan nodded. "An unfortunate countenance. My mother was the sweetest woman. So patient and kind, but I'd see her face and wonder, 'Why is she so angry?' My daughter inherited the look. Sometimes I'll watch her sitting, doing nothing, and wonder if she's plotting my death."

Colleen ate the last muffin bite.

"Why are you running for school board, Susan?"

Susan smiled as she shook her head. "I want to say for the children, but the truth is I hate my neighbor. Her name is Minnie. Can you believe that? Minnie? She's a teacher at Washington Elementary and I want her to fear me." She shrugged.

"That's as good a reason as any," Colleen said, finally realizing whom Susan's husband was having an affair with.

She ordered another muffin.

@

Colleen waited for Jimmy on her front porch. Frances Burnish walked by with her dog. She tied the leash to a light post and sat next to Colleen. She pulled a flask from her cleavage. "It's vodka."

"Dirty?"

"Just my mind."

They passed it back and forth several times.

Frances winked. "Can't win the day sober."

Colleen laughed. She rested her head on Frances' shoulder. "Do you miss Milton?"

"That dumpster shaped know-it-all?" Her voice went high. "More than he could've ever guessed."

Colleen took a swig. "I miss 'The Kellermans,' you know, the title. The idea. The positivity of introducing a collective. But I don't miss Phil."

"Me either."

Frances' dog didn't even flinch when a squirrel ran up to him.

"Do I have a mean looking face?" Colleen asked.

Frances slipped the flask into her cleavage. "Take some advice from me, someone who looks like they were conceived and born and raised in a used car lot: enjoy your threatening beauty. It's power." She undid the leash and said she'd taught her dog a new trick. "President." The dog ran to Lance Reynolds' lawn and squatted. "I call it the 'Trump Dump. I'm not cleaning that up either. Gimme one of your damn 'Eyesore' notifications, Frau Kellerman. See if I give a shit." She laughed and goose-stepped home.

Still waiting, one glass of Merlot became three. Across the street, Nikki Longstreth parked her car. Jimmy exited. He passed Colleen. She sipped her wine. The toilet flushed. He jumped off the porch and waved without looking back.

"Where you off to?"

When he turned, he had a cookie in his mouth. He snapped off a bite. "Got a lame, school thing. Getting extra credit for Worth's AP Lang class though."

Stratus clouds hovered in the sky. She swirled her wine.

"Why'd you steal my signs, Jimmy?"

Jimmy silently protested Colleen's perfectly still face. He looked past the Longstreths, to the woods, then back at her face. He scratched his neck and ran his tongue over his teeth.

"You make such a big deal out of everything?"

"Big deal?"

"It couldn't just be one sign in our yard. It had to be a sign in every yard." He made a violent gesture at the Peephole. "Every mailbox needs to be the same. Christmas lights must be red around the trunks and white everywhere else. 'Eyesore' this. 'Eyesore' that. How long before you turn the entire school district into an expanded Peephole?" He shook his head. "You're just so extra. All the time. Just once I'd wish you'd be anything but this clichéd suburbanite. I mean . . ." He grunted. "When you found out the signs were missing, that's how you should've acted when Dad left."

Jimmy huffed.

"Were you high when you took the signs?"

"Are you drunk right now?"

"I know that's why you went to Kinkos. You went to see that worker. Not to help me. He reeked of it. How much are you smoking?"

"Unbelievable. Don't be my mom, right now, okay? Just, uh, go do what you do. Go walk the perimeter. Drink a bottle of red. Make sure everyone has the right type of door wreath or something."

Across the street, Nikki Longstreth exited her house. She had a streak of red and a streak of green in her white-blonde hair. She dressed like a Catholic schoolgirl seeking detention. Sooner or later the burlesque Crayola-haired-carousel would tip the fetish scale in the wrong balance and Jimmy would begin screwing her, if he wasn't already.

"I love you, Jimmy" Colleen whispered, as Nikki walked up the driveway. "Even when you make me cry myself to sleep, I still love you."

Nikki pointed at Jimmy. "You ready?"

Colleen gave a fake smile. "Nikki, off to confession?"

"Good one." She punched Jimmy in the arm. "No, we're off to the high school poetry slam. Hosted by me, cuz, I'm awesome." Jimmy shot her a look. "Okay, okay. Co-hosting. Jimmy's my partner in crime. And hopefully some other kids'll show, or else it'll just be Jimmy and me reading our stuff to an empty room." She looked at Jimmy and shrugged. "You coming to the show, Mrs. Kellerman?"

"Jesus, Nikki. Are you serious right now?"

"Should I add a streak of purple before I go?" Colleen said, touching her hair.

"Nah. That new look is hot enough. Perfect shape for your face."

Jimmy tugged her arm. "Let's get some grub before the show."

"I'll save you a seat, Mrs. Kellerman."

And they were gone.

She finished another glass of wine and watched the sunset. She stood but didn't go inside. Instead, she marched away from the cul-de-sac, away from her empty house, away from the Peephole, towards the train tracks. When she got there, Don Longstreth was sitting on a log, a vape pen in his hand. He took a hit and stared at the sky.

"Don?"

His eyes went wide, but after seeing Colleen, he couldn't stop laughing. "*Guten tag, Frau.*" He laughed and held out the vape pen. "Never got the fascist reference to you. You're more of a communist gal."

"Thanks, I guess," she said, eyeing the device.

"Go on, but be careful. It's not like when we were kids. This is government grade. Pure THC distillate. Kids today don't have to want for anything." He coughed. "Sure, they're emotionally and psychologically damaged beyond repair and will forever remain children disguised as adults, but, they won't be aware of it. Assholes." He offered the vape pen to Colleen. "We bust a kid about ten times a day for these. I've learned all about them. Even how to clean it for pot use so there are no traces of nicotine." He took a hit. "Just a father looking out for his daughter."

"Ten times a day?"

"Not always for pot. They use it for the nicotine they claim they aren't addicted to. Kids are stupid."

"You take that from a student?"

He laughed as he exhaled. "This is Nikki's. Or Junior's." He shrugged. "This is their smoking spot. I have no idea where they got the THC. Knew they wouldn't be here tonight. Don't worry. They don't mess with the flavored nicotine pod nonsense. They just smoke this. Guess we raised them right."

Colleen sat next to him. She held the vape pen, unsure what to do with it.

"Just take a hit." She told him she was already drunk. "Perfect." He nudged her side. She'd never smoked marijuana before. She caught her husband smoking it once in the garage and threatened to call the police.

She handed it back to Don. She didn't know if it did anything.

"You weren't invited to the poetry thing either?"

"It's like I'm living with a stranger."

"Better than terrorist rule."

Colleen nodded. She walked to her signs and dug her hand in the leaves and yanked on a wire. She stuck the sign in the ground.

"I swear I didn't' do that."

"Jim . . . Junior did it."

She looked at her sign, and hit the vape pen again.

"Slow down first-timer."

"In high school, I was on homecoming court. Sara Gill won, but standing there in front of everyone, before her name was called, was nice." She ran her hands along the sign. "Sometimes I wish I could be trapped in that moment. Standing there before I lost. It was nice. Really, really nice."

"You're an odd one, Colleen Kellerman." He smiled at her.

"I try so hard not to be. Being odd is so noticeable." She laughed and kept laughing until her face hurt. She handed the vape pen back to Don. He took one last hit. "If they only knew I stole their stash." He laughed and placed the vape pen in a baggie.

"You aren't going to take it? You're just going to let them smoke?"

"I'm worried if I do, she'll stop talking to me."

Don dropped the baggie in a hole on top of a blue blanket stuffed in a big baggie.

"I can't get Junior to clean his room, but he'll come out here and dig a three-foot-deep hole?"

"Sounds about right." Don picked up a dead bush and stuffed it on the hole. Colleen pointed to where she saw the blanket.

"You think our kids are having sex."

"I'm sure she's having sex, but not with Junior."

"What's wrong with Junior?"

"Nothing. Nothing at all."

Don dug his hands into the leaves and pulled out a sign. He was careful about removing the leaves, and like Colleen, he rubbed his hands across the tight plastic as if to heighten its sheen. "Good sign. Patriotic." Don placed the sign under his right arm and cupped her face in his hands. "I like you like this. Relaxed. Non-expressive. Real."

"You're stoned."

"I am."

When Don didn't move, she placed her hands on his face. Don had a kind face, the face that lets you merge into traffic. He placed his hands on her face. For some time, they stood in the stillness, holding faces.

"I think I want to kiss you," Don said.

"Okay," Colleen said.

Without moving their hands, Don kissed her. She kissed him back. Don backed away, so did Colleen, but neither lowered their hands.

"One time," Don said, "I was driving in northern Arizona at night. I was all by myself. No one else on the road. A light shot across the sky. Then another. I stopped the car, got out, and for two minutes witnessed a meteor shower. This beautiful, unsuspected moment, made the curiosities of the universe enough to want to live all of life."

Colleen grabbed his hands and together they held her resting face.

"You're so stoned."

Don nodded. He helped the dying bush look part of the natural plain. Before he left, he grabbed a sign and said, "You got my vote."

She pulled out the other signs and pushed them into the dirt, forming a circle around the bush. "I'll take the heat for this one. Your daughter can still love you," she said, giggling, as she trudged back toward the cul-de-sac, the Peephole, home.

Don Longstreth stuck her sign in his yard. She watched him go inside and then he appeared in the window. She waved. He waved back. He turned off his light and disappeared into his dark house.

She breathed in the night spring air. This was her favorite time of year. First, the tulips blossomed. Then the grass greened. Then the leaves bloomed. She didn't have to encourage one plant or one blade of grass or one flower to act. It just happened. Naturally.

She panted as she entered her house. She ate smart, so she never had to work out, not that swinging her campaign sign to obliterate Lance's tulips and to rip at the ivy crawling up the brick façade constituted a workout, but it tested her aerobic endurance. She poured the rest of the merlot into a pint glass and entered Junior's bathroom. The electric razor she'd gotten him for Christmas due to his insistence was unopened in a drawer. Her blonde hair fell to the floor. It was effortless, like clearing bubbles atop bath water. She rubbed her hands over her stubbly scalp then kissed her reflection. "You cannot stop the multitude from whispering. Gifting them your ears empowers their judgment." She updated her profile picture on Facebook as she walked to her bedroom, leaving the mess for Junior.

# Higher Ground

AFTER SMOKING A little bud she'd purchased from Wes, a man-child from the west side who seemed to linger in the school hallways but never enter a classroom, Nikki lay on her bed, and tried to convince herself she wouldn't log-in as LOSTSOUL2000, but this was becoming a nightly lie.

—FratBOYzRULE: How much for a flash bb?

—RUSHfan4ever: u still seeing that assclown?

She kept quiet, staring at her digital reflection, her cartoonish hair-dye adulterating a genetic gift, her mother's beautiful blonde hair. A red bra strap exposed under a sweatshirt cut at the neck, making it loose at the shoulders. The word PINK embossed on the front in blue. Black eyeliner outlined her green eyes reading messages from the 1293 people watching.

—stormtroopersfuk2: wood luv to cu smile.

Her fragile bird-like limbs were asked to: unclasp, type, play, rub, insert, spread, squirt, touch toes, finger.

—RUSHfan4ever: cum'on. Jizz tell me how to get at you, bb

Cambate.com made a deposit each month to her checking account—sixty cents on the dollar. Easy money. Thousands of dollars a month. Her dad's naivety allowed him to believe she'd made this money serving tables at an Italian restaurant. No doubt she could've earned more, but she'd made rules for herself: No nudity. No touching. No blown kisses. No requests of any kind.

Most nights she simply gave empty gazes promulgating attraction, becoming a mystery, a modern-day chat-room Mona Lisa on display for the perverted analysts of the world to dissect and discuss and argue and agree and admire and hate and care and love and cherish and keep but never have.

—RUSHfan4ever: u no I luv u right?

—RUSHfan4ever: do anything 4 you ;)

A creak in the hallway floorboards moved her vacant eyes away from the screen, a dangerous hope, waiting for the door-knob to turn before things went too far, but the only rotation in the house seemed to be a pattern of pain—pain she wanted to inflict on someone else with ballooning desire. Maybe then she'd feel something new, curious if compunction was still a part of her emotional compound since all she thought about anymore was revenge.

A door down the hall shut. Thinking how lonely and heartbroken her dad had become since her mom had left them both for God made her cry. Through her tears she sang the song her mom hummed incessantly the week before she left:

"My heart has no desire to stay
Where doubts arise and fears dismay;
Though some may dwell where those abound,
My prayer, my aim, is higher ground."
*Bing! Bing! Bing!* The tips came pouring in.

—RUSHfan4ever: better than Geddy Lee! PM me! Got a pic for u.

—humpNrun: so beautiful! sing something else. please.

The perverts enjoyed her gospel and continued to tip and write: "Hallelujah" and "Praise be topless" and "Part those legs" and "Get on your knees and show penance," and so on and so on until she logged-off as LOSTSOUL2000.

@

Nikki waited for hunger to strike. Summer burdened her with too much free time. Too much time to think. To create. To murder. To recreate, or so echoed in her head after reading T.S. Eliot to end the year in Mr. Weber's Advanced American Literature class. She thought about making "Missing" posters for Cinna, their dog, who had run away a few days ago, but she never loved the dog. She got it after her mom left and all the dog did was remind her of that. School had only been out a week and she'd already read her summer work for AP Literature and written the accompanying analytical papers. She was frustrated how Jay Gatsby's oblivious self-deception spawned his own destruction and found Professor Humbert Humbert from Nabokov's *Lolita* both despicable and fascinating. Even though Humbert Humbert reminded her of Lance, she begrudgingly empathized with him, as Nabokov had a way of humanizing the despicable Professor, something that Lance had yet to do for himself.

Too bored to work, she called a server to cover her shift. She'd never called off work without a replacement. She wouldn't do that to Mr. Scuro, especially since his son died earlier in the year on Valentine's Day while serving in Afghanistan. She didn't know what to say to Mr. Scuro after hearing the news. Since then his eyes seemed to be stuck in a wistful sorrowfulness transforming him to look like a crass, soulless animation. She tried to capture that look while she cammed, but no matter how desperate and hollow she tried to portray herself, there was still a spark to her eye, a promised incendiary desire that continued to lure the perverts.

After eating an entire big bag of Fritos, she texted Jimmy—the boy who lived across the street—asking to meet at the secret garden. She took a shower and used pomegranate conditioner and body lotion. She liked her skin and hair matching smells, offering this unity to summer air. The simplistic thought of the aligned fragrance made her smile, a small, solitary reaction she couldn't control. She put on a red tank top and jean shorts and exited the sliding back door, heading towards the woods behind her house.

Jimmy stood against a tree, scribbling something in his Moleskine. He always looked so fucking cool. They'd made-out a few months ago after they had co-hosted a Poetry Slam event at their school. She wanted to feel a promise of something more, but it only felt like she was kissing him as practice, sending her right back to Lance. She wished her sex drive wasn't so healthy. A few of her girlfriends never talked about sex, as if it wasn't of any interest. They seemed happy.

Jimmy closed the Moleskine and stuffed it in his back pocket. He wore black skinny jeans and a frayed t-shirt with a llama on it. She hated that shirt like he was trying too hard to be hip or artistic or non-commercial or whatever.

"Thought you were working tonight." He sat down on a blanket, the one they would roll up and stuff into in a large purple Ziploc plastic bag and shove in a hole when they left. The one she sometimes used with Lance.

"Called off," Nikki said, wanting to sit down next to Jimmy, but choosing not to.

"About time you blow off Scuro. Guy has like a weird hold over you." Jimmy swallowed, which bobbed his Adam's apple up and down. After a short pause, he said, "We smoking?"

Nikki reached to her back pocket and pulled out the baggy she'd bought from Wes. Jimmy turned over a big rock and reached into a hole and pulled out a baggy with a pipe and lighter in it. As he packed the pipe he said he missed using the vape pen, but they couldn't score anymore THC distillate. They both accused the other of smoking their last one without sharing. He held the first hit out for Nikki. She shook her head. Jimmy shrugged, lit the pipe and inhaled.

"I'm seeing someone," Nikki said, looking down, never having spoken about Lance, except on her cam chats.

"Good for you,"

Jimmy again offered her the pipe. Again, she refused.

"I'm thinking of ending it though."

Jimmy didn't respond to her remark. She sat down on the rock that had hidden the pipe but felt bumps and ridges in all the wrong places. She stared at the meticulously stretched blanket. When Lance unrolled it, she always felt bunches of fabric on her back as he writhed on top of her.

"My dad's taking me to the Gallery Hop next Saturday," Jimmy said, sounding apathetic as if spending time with his dad was a punishment.

Like Nikki's mom, Jimmy's dad just one day disappeared. But he came back. Nikki's mom had been gone almost a year now and the only time Nikki heard from her was through random post-cards, which she kept locked away in the order she'd received them in the bottom of her desk drawer. All of them had a cross or a church or a Bible verse or some other religious propaganda on it that made Nikki want to throw-up.

"You wanna come? My dad's trying really hard to be cool. He'll probably buy us beer."

Nikki stared at the knothole in the maple tree behind Jimmy. She wondered what had happened to the limb that had died and fallen off to create it. Regardless of this blemish, the tree still soared, its leaves a proud green. She searched the ground for the limb that became kindling and felt sad for it.

She looked at the Moleskine sticking out of the back of Jimmy's pocket.

"Read one," she said.

Jimmy's eyebrows raised.

"A poem for a truth."

She grabbed the pipe and took a hit.

"Okay," she said, picking flakes off her tongue.

"If you could ask me anything, what would it be?"

She thought of RUSHfan4ever's confession.

"Would you kill for me?"

"What's wrong with you?" Jimmy said, standing, walking backward.

"What?"

"That's just a morbid, fucking question."

"What did you think I'd ask?"

He shrugged. "If I hooked up with Nate Edwards or not."

Jimmy was pansexual. Once she referred to Jimmy as bisexual and he walked off in a huff and said it was like she didn't even try to get him.

"I don't really care if you did or not, but you seem like you really want to tell me that you did, so, go ahead, give me all the graphic details."

He snorted something that sounded like "unbelievable" under his breath and flipped the pages in his Moleskine.

"Secret garden, secret garden
Open up and swallow me
and wilt all my misery
Cut the roots and turn me loose
Fertilize this blossoming bruise
Extirpate my hopeless buds
inhale all of the oxygen
and prune my burgeoning stems
Secret garden, secret garden
open up and swallow me."

She'd named this place their "secret garden" because it was the place they would never keep secrets, but since they had kissed and Jimmy felt her up, and she rubbed him over his jeans, all she wanted to do was lie to him.

Jimmy shook the leaves off the bottom of the blanket before rolling it up.

Lance never swept off the leaves.

"So, I'm a bitch. But if you want me to have an actual epiphany—"

"Being mean isn't your thing, Nikki. Now, my mom knows how to be a bitch. But you being a bitch is pathetic to watch." He struggled to get the blanket in the plastic bag. "And stop changing your hair color. It's blonde. It's not that!" He pointed at her hair, which was light pink with green streaks.

He threw the blanket down and walked past her. He told her to text when she didn't suck anymore. She mumbled under her breath she didn't know when that would be. As his footsteps trailed away, she rolled up the blanket, feeling the stains, the ones Jimmy seemed to never notice.

"What are your plans for the summer?" her dad asked, not looking up, as he sliced into his open-faced turkey sandwich from Bob Evans.

"Work at The Florentine." She tried to cut a single piece of rice. "Work on a tan." She flattened a piece of chicken with her fork. "Commit murder."

Her dad laughed. "If you want to go all serial, I have a few names for you." He took a bite of the sandwich. "I saw Robbins assigned Nabokov for summer reading. Want to talk about it? It's pretty intense. 'Fire of my loins' and all that." He leaned toward her.

"It's about a grown man sodomizing a twelve-year-old. What's to talk about?"

"That was the original tag line," he said, smiling, but stopped when Nikki turned to stare at the wall. If the walls hadn't been there, she would have been looking at Lance's house. She thought of his boyish grin, the one he used to be both bad and forgiven. She wanted to take a box cutter to the corners of his mouth and watch his head unfold the next time he tried it on her.

"Conducting a chicken autopsy?" her dad said, nodding at her plate.

She wanted to laugh but was out of practice in doing so. Her dad used to be funny and charming and sarcastic, maybe he still was, but he looked so different. His clothes seem to hang off him now. He'd lost at least thirty pounds.

"Nikki?"

She looked at a bloody vein in the chicken and tried to remove it with her fork, and continued to do so until she sensed her Dad deflect his stare.

@

After logging in as LOSTSOUL2000, she set the laptop on her bed and folded her laundry. When she did normal things, the tips were good. One of the biggest tip nights she ever had was narrating her calculus homework. Each time she successfully answered a problem it paraded tips. *Bing! Bing! Bing!*

After she put her clothes away, she took out the small stack of postcards from her bottom desk drawer. The last one was from Montgomery, Alabama. She knew nothing about Montgomery, so she Googled it and discovered it was the second most religious city in the United States—she assumed everywhere in Utah was tied for first. Shortly before abandoning her family, Nikki relented to her mother's requests and attended a revival church service with her. Before the Reverend John Paul's *Evangelical Calling* came to the Franklin County Fairgrounds, Nikki had only been to church on Christmas Eve and Easter. That day she went solely to live tweet her mom's uninhibited involvement with such a spectacle, but once she saw her mother merge with the congregation, she couldn't mock her. The true revival was in her mom's beauty and youth and affability, turning her into a stranger. At the end of the sermon, Nikki had joined the congregation in the "Amens" and "Hallelujahs" chanting in unison, attempting to lure her mother's admiration, but she never took her eyes off Reverend John Paul.

"Rejoice in hope, be patient in tribulation, be constant in prayer: Romans 12:12," was in bold letters over the Church of the Holy Comforter in Montgomery, Alabama. Handwritten on the back was: I'm learning to play tambourine. Love, Mom.

She read all the postcards aloud.

*Bing! Bing! Bing!*

She began to cry.

*Bing! Bing! Bing!*

She crawled onto the bed and closed her eyes, knowing if she fell asleep on camera at just the right angle, the tips would keep coming.

@

It was almost three in the morning when a text message woke her:

Lance: Still on this week?

Lance didn't take notice of Nikki until the cul-de-sac had learned about her mother's leaving. At first, she'd refused Lance's come-ons—one in which he'd called the space between her legs the Holy Grail—but his desperate persistence gave her a power she wanted to wield and control and abuse and sustain. The way he looked at her made her think, *I can get away with anything.* So, one night, after the funeral of Frances Burnish's husband—the woman who lives across the street—much to the jubilant shock of

137

Lance, she didn't back away from him. And oh the power! Being with Lance was void of the self-consciousness that accompanied sex within her social group. She didn't have to worry about rumors or stories or glares in the hallways or her dad finding out through work gossip—he worked as a guidance counselor at her school. And the more vulgar and upfront Lance Reynolds was with what he wanted, the freer she felt. She craved his honesty and he gave her this dirty, wonderful secret, and oh the power! Lance was engaged. Lance made small talk with her dad at parties. Lance was rumored to have had an affair with Jimmy's mom. Lance lived three houses down. Lance was: Something to do. Something to dictate. Something to binge. Something to submit to. Something to pass the time. Something to distract. Lance was a real-life *Netflix*.

She moved to the window and looked at Vintage Woods Court and wondered how insignificant it must be in relation to the galaxy; how her mother was a part of the galaxy, yet not a part of her life; how Jimmy was probably screwing Nate Edwards; how her tryst with Lance wasn't a ripple worth a damn in the scheme of the universe, so why stop it; how people died all the time, yet the universe kept expanding, charging through its infinite space, never running out of real estate, how there was not a sillier thought than to assume her pain was important in the grand scheme.

She answered Lance's text, closed the draperies, and found her way back to bed.

@

The mail carrier closed the mailbox and gave Nikki a thumbs-up. The postcard was from Louisiana. No specific city. No Bible verse. Just a cartoon depiction of the state with Mardi Gras beads, an alligator, gumbo, and a football on the front. There wasn't a note, just her signature in cursive: Mom.

Across the street, Frances Burnish took the mail from the mail carrier. Nikki waited for the mail truck to pass before crossing.

Frances sifted through the mail, cursing as she did so. "If it's not a bill, it's junk mail for my dead husband." She held up three advertisements pointing at the "Mr." part. "It's like the local lawn services conspired to remind me I'm a widow, while simultane-ously reviving sexism. Like a woman can't make a homeowner's choice concerning grass. Assholes of the world unite. Jesus Christ on a pogo-stick, I tell you what."

Nikki never knew if the comedy was intentional, but Frances was the funniest person she knew. Frances had taken an interest in Nikki over that past few months, buying her things, talking about the Bible, giving her sips of bourbon, because, "it was the polite thing to do." Sometimes when she was with Frances, she'd laugh so hard she'd remember all those wonderful times with her father and mother, back before those evangelicals knocked on their door.

Frances moved her eyes from her mail to Nikki.

"You look like a corpse that can't sleep, kid. Spill it."

"Spill what?"

"Sorry kiddo, your hips, lips, and fingertips don't bewitch me." Frances pointed at Nikki's house. "I don't sleep much, and from what I gather, neither do you. Why is the light always on in your window?"

Without thinking, she said, "I webcam for money."

"I'm not sure what that means, but it sounds problematic." Frances took a cigarette from her pocket and inhaled, although she never lit it. "You may not believe this, but when I was your age, I was a knock-out, much like you are now. Not my face, mind you, my face has always been 'B' side, but my curves and my legs. They got attention." Frances looked at Lance's house. "A pretty, well-constructed young female—regardless of age—makes men stupid. Just plain stupid." She took another hit of the unlit cigarette, then dropped it and smashed it with her foot.

"I think it just makes them weird."

Nikki stared at Lance's house, wondering what it looked like inside. There had been a few hotel rooms, but mostly Lance told Nikki to meet him at homes for sale. Being a realtor, Lance arranged for the house to be empty and they'd spend these fabri-cated moments having sex on strangers' beds, timing their rela-tionship to half-hour increments.

"Weird I can handle. Stupid is the problem." Frances gushed a rueful laugh. "Sadly, we seem to counter stupid with stupid—webcamming for money—now you go ahead and ask me what stupid plus stupid equals."

She asked.

"Pain."

@

At two in the morning, she logged off and put on a sweatshirt. Her dad's snores dissipated as she reached the bottom of the stairs. She exited through the sliding door in the kitchen and made her way towards the secret garden.

The moon was full and bright so she didn't need to use the flashlight app on her phone. She missed all the dead leaves and twigs, startling Lance who was leaning against a tree, a bottle of champagne in his hand. He popped the cork and laughed as the champagne sprayed everywhere. He took a swig and held it out for her.

"This is for you, Nikki-baby," Lance said, careless with the champagne, as it ran down his chin. His synthetic teeth shone brightly under the dark canopy. "Sorry for this to be so late. The fiancée wasn't on-call until midnight. Before that she had me look over fifty different fonts trying to pick out wedding invitations." He moved towards her. "It was hard to concentrate on something so pointless, knowing I'd be licking your sweet nectar."

Lance handed her the bottle. Champagne bottles always felt so heavy. Nikki noticed this while serving. Wine bottles felt how they looked, but champagne bottles were deceivingly dense. She took a sip and thought how the bottle would make a good truncheon.

"Don't make that face, Nikki-baby." Lance cupped his hand under her chin. "Next week I'll find a nice place. One of those mansions on the Scioto. Promise."

She gripped the neck of the champagne bottle.

"That's an eighty-dollar bottle of champagne. At least try it."

He loved to mention the cost of things. She moved past him, towards the opening in the trees, where the moonlight was brightest.

"Do you ever feel guilty, Lance?"

"Guilty? About sex?" He shook his head. "I love women, Nikki. All kinds of women." He looked at her. "I won't ever feel guilty over something I love."

He moved to her. Even in the cover of the night, his motion was languid and sensual, something she couldn't refuse. As they embraced, she chose not to share with him that this was goodbye, and as the rolls of fabric pushed in her back, she tried to convince herself that she wasn't going to miss it.

@

An hour later, she opened her LOSTSOUL2000 profile. There was a congratulatory note from the webmasters. She now had over a thousand followers. At their suggestion a few months ago, she'd created a PO box so her more ardent fans could send her gifts. If she started undressing and following fan requests she could pay for college.

She turned her back to the web camera and opened the window. The cool, night air washed over her. She pulled her sweatshirt up to her chin. *Bing! Bing! Bing!* Goosebumps spread across her chest. She wondered if Mrs. Burnish saw. She removed the sweatshirt and turned around, giving herself a hand bra.

*Bing! Bing! Bing!*

The wind knocked the blind's cord against the wall in a quick, rhythmic pattern. With her left arm draped over her breasts, she unlocked the bottom drawer with her free hand and pulled out the postcards. The cord continued to bop. The scent of a promised summer rain wafted in. She fanned out the postcards, creating a circle. She closed her eyes and patted the postcards against her hip, matching the rhythm of the cord. *Bing! Bing! Bing!* She hummed that song—the one her mother sang before she left—and danced like her mother did that day at the fairgrounds, unaware of the figure standing in her doorway.

# The Scratch

H IS WIFE RUBBED her pregnant stomach as she walked into the fourth bedroom. He moved to the window and looked at the woods beyond the neighborhood. "It could be an office," she said. "Maybe you'll start writing again." The realtor reminded her that there was an office on the first floor, but that room could also become a sitting room because, with this much space, the options seemed endless.

After the realtor left to give them privacy, she twirled in the kitchen, arms out, letting go of her five-month baby bump. "It's a steal," she said, pointing to the gourmet double ovens. "How can we say no?" Her smile beckoned Sean to hug her, so he did. She placed her head on his chest and whispered, "Fresh start." She mimicked his heartbeat by tapping his chest, and then she tapped slower—this is something she'd done over the years to calm him, or as she put it, *to not fight with reason.* "Don't you think the dark coffee floorboards perfectly complement the java cabinets? It's even got a granite island. I could do food prepping here. Hang some pots and pans above it. It'll look like we're hosting a cooking show! Oh, think of what we could create in here!"

Lance Reynolds, their realtor, paced the front porch, talking on his cell. All Sean knew about Lance Reynolds was that he was pleasant, engaged, and good at his job; yet, he sensed maliciousness beneath that affability cloak. But Ellen liked him and shushed Sean anytime he tried to talk about the mystery of Lance Reynolds.

"What do you think?" Lance opened his arms wide. "Pretty wonderful, right?" He grinned, flashing his fake teeth. Ellen nodded. Sean didn't reply. "As you know, I live right there," Lance pointed to the house at the base of the cul-de-sac. "I only bring clients here that I can one day see as my neighbors." He placed his hand over his heart. "My friends." He strolled to Sean and Ellen. "Howard Havenshaw, the guy who used to live here, just one day disappeared. Moved somewhere else. Don't know where. West maybe." He shrugged. "Weeks later he hired movers. He contacted me sometime after and told me he's willing to lose money on the house, as long as the people moving in were high caliber. Truth be known, I've only shown this to two other couples. And well, after vetting them, they didn't make Howard's cut."

"Vetting? Are we running for Congress?" Sean said.

"I find it fascinating," Ellen said. "Very unusual for us to be involved in something so secretive and interesting."

"It's odd." Sean tapped the stone façade, expecting it to crumble.

"Sean, I get your apprehension. I do. Mr. Havenshaw was an Army man. Served like three or four tours in Vietnam. I don't think he's eccentric, just someone who's all about honor. 'Be all you can be.' 'The right stuff.' That type of mentality." Lance shrugged. "Between you and me, the neighbors are getting restless. This is a pretty tight-knit street. An empty house at the front for too long gives the wrong impression. Believe me. We are the opposite of unwelcoming."

They walked down the front porch steps. A naked flagpole stood in the front yard. Sean examined the house's exterior, Hardie Plank. Aside from Lance's house—which was all brick—the rest were stucco. "Did he have to replace the stucco?" He rambled about the dangers of mold. Ellen cut him off.

"No issues of mold. Promise. I didn't have issues with mold either, just felt like all brick looked better. More classic."

"So all the houses used to be stucco?"

Lance nodded. "One day people were here, working on Howard's home." Lance smiled, showing those veneers that looked so good on his business card. "Howard was a war hero. Hardie Plank is the best product out there. Maybe he wanted to protect the new owners. Keep them safe. Keep *you* safe."

"Remodeling a home that doesn't need it? Investing thousands and thousands in something with no possible return on that investment? Leaving the space empty?" He shot Ellen a look. "Does any of this make sense to you?"

"Listen," Lance said, stepping forward. "I'll have the inspector come out ASAP. If he finds something wrong, then we'll move on, and look in Worthington like you'd suggested." Lance smiled. Sean assumed that smile had gotten him a lot of favors people didn't want to give him.

"None of this feels right." Sean shook his head. "Vetted?" Ellen grabbed Sean's hand.

"Don't take it personally," Lance said. "Besides, if Howard Havenshaw gives you guys a Google search, what's he going to find? That you both give back to the community by teaching high school? These days, high school teachers have to be more honest than the Pope."

The first hit on Google wasn't about them being teachers. Sean knew that for sure.

He mumbled something no one understood and wandered to the side of the house. He pressed his hand against the Hardie Plank and snorted. Ellen sat on the front steps and fanned herself with her hand, holding her belly with the other.

*Try not to overthink it.*

Their couples' counselor introduced this phrase to them four months ago. Ellen used it as a trigger, as if to hypnotize Sean into complacency.

"Here's an idea," Lance said. "Colleen Kellerman, who lives next door there, throws these wonderful cul-de-sac parties. She calls them Peephole Parties."

"Why?" Ellen asked.

"She saw our street once flying back from Chicago and she said it looked just like a peephole."

"That's adorable."

"I think so too, Ellen. I think so too." Lance held his smile for a few seconds, making Ellen smile too. Sean leaned against the side of the house, listening. "Colleen's having a July Fourth bash this Saturday. You'll love Colleen. She's a School Board Member. We are very pro public education on this street."

"She sounds important."

"Indeed she is, Ellen." Lance pointed. "We place cones at the front of the cul-de-sac and we roll our grills out to the street. Why not stop by? Meet the neighbors. Get a feel for the street."

Sean felt like he was rushing fraternities all over again. He could never tell if the guys in the fraternity genuinely liked him or sought him for diversity or offered pleasantries as placation so they didn't seem racist.

A plane flew overhead. After it passed, he could hear Ellen breathing. It was steady and rhythmic, like when she used Lamaze with the delivery of their first child before she realized it didn't work and demanded drugs.

Lance pointed to Ellen's belly and then across the street. "Zak and Celia Turner just announced they're expecting. They live next to me on the right. I believe they are due early November."

"That is so close to our date!" Ellen said, nudging Sean.

"And, I believe the Whitings, who live there, are also expecting."

"Really?" Ellen said.

"Sounds like that future whippersnapper of yours has built-in best friends."

Sean scanned the street. It was much nicer than their current neighborhood. A spider crawled up the side of the house. Sean stepped back. He'd hadn't noticed the web connecting the tree and the gutter. He itched all over, wondering what else he'd missed.

@

Their first child's name had been Daniel. Howard Havenshaw could learn this from a Google search.

While pregnant Ellen had an image of this beautiful boy, with profuse black curls, with brown eyes like fresh turned over soil. In looking at pictures in Sean's family albums, she discovered this imagined child. She turned it over: *Daniel, Age 2.* Sean had no idea who the boy was or why it was with his mother's pictures.

"It's a sign," Ellen said. "We'll name him Daniel, and call him Danny. Maybe the name will give him those curls." And it did.

Seven months after Danny was born, when the anxiety about Sudden Infant Death Syndrome had passed, Danny went to sleep one night and never woke up. While Ellen screamed, Sean peeled back his son's cold eyelid, to see a little sliver of light brown circling his dilated pupil. And now, their home, the one Ellen had labeled a dream home, seemed unlivable. He couldn't walk by the room at the top of the stairs without thinking about his little still body looking as if he'd never been real.

Ellen was already pregnant when Danny died. When she told him Danny would be a big brother, Sean laughed and said, "But you're still breastfeeding." Ellen's first pregnancy made him nervous, and after Danny was born, the terror didn't relent: *How can I protect something so helpless? Who am I?* When Ellen was too tired to breastfeed, and Sean fed Danny bottles in the morning darkness, he felt like bursting. He wasn't ready for fatherhood, and couldn't stop wondering how this new role would change him, his life. That unknown haunted him, so much so, when Danny died, he felt responsible, as if any minute the authorities would barge in and arrest him.

@

It was still dark when the scratching woke Sean. The promise of a hangover panged as he squinted at the ceiling. Had he really drunk that much last night? His wife lay on her side, snoring. He nudged her.

"What?" she said.

"Listen!"

"It's still dark out. What time is it?"

"Shh," he said. "Just listen."

*Scratch. Scratch. Scratch.*

"Hear that?" He pointed up.

"Yes." She put her head on the pillow. "Infestation? Another reason to move."

He stood on the bed. With their ceilings only eight feet high, he knocked and the scratching grew louder. He jumped off the bed and the scratching followed him. When he stopped. It stopped. Like a sound shadow.

"Are you seeing this?"

"Yes," she sighed. "Rodents. Or worse!" She sat up, suddenly alert. "We need to call someone today! If the Havenshaw place passes inspection, it won't mean anything if our house doesn't."

Sean folded his arms. "I don't think it's an animal. It's like it's . . ."

"What else could it be?"

His stare silenced her. In the bathroom, he noticed a faint sound above him. Then, as he walked back to bed, something in the ceiling scraped in gentle rhythms, mirroring his movement.

Ellen held out her arms. "Cuddle me until we have to absolutely get up," she said. He lay down and she put her head on his shoulder. He stroked her hair, well after his arm grew tired.

"I really like that house, Sean. It's a good school district, better than the one we teach in. I know the thing with the owner is weird, but so what? I can't be in this house when this baby is born. We only have one other bedroom upstairs. We were going to have to move anyway." Her voice grew soft as she breathed heavy.

Their therapist had stated tears are a trigger of guilt and people liked to wallow in that guilt to feel self-pity as to feel something. For Sean, their tears were for the sadness of losing a child. He would cry how and when he pleased and feel what he wanted to feel. But Ellen, she wanted to think their therapist had magic in his words, so she followed them blindly.

"I'll admit. It's pretty perfect," Sean said, thinking nothing would ever be perfect again.

"It is perfect, isn't it? Forget the weirdness attached to it. Try not to overthink it." She nestled her head onto his shoulder, but couldn't get situated. "I feel like I grew overnight." He motioned for her to turn around. She obliged and he rubbed her shoulders. A few minutes later, the scratching came back.

"Ellen?"

"I hear it too." She squeezed him. "I don't care if we have two mortgages. We're moving."

They never discussed why they'd yet to officially put their house on the market. In the morning, before he adjusted to the day, Sean would forget and expect to hear cooing or laughing or crying. Each time Sean walked by his son's closed door, he felt further from Ellen, further from any memory of Danny, further from everything.

The scratching grew louder. "I'm calling an exterminator." She grabbed her phone. Sean grabbed her leg.

"What if it's not a critter?" Sean asked, suddenly filled with a hope he didn't quite understand. On their first date, they felt connected with how they both let down their parents by not being religious or spiritual.

"It's probably chewing through our wires. Who knows what that would cost?"

If it were a rodent, it could create a fire hazard by gnawing on the wiring. Sean had a buddy, Kurt, who was a fireman in Cincinnati. He used him as a source for research for his unpublished novel, which was really just an allegory on the inner city. Fires started for all kinds of reasons, a mouse in the ceiling was as good as any. Still, Sean couldn't shake the sense that the scratching was important, a coded message: *Don't sell.*

@

The exterminator exited the attic. "I've searched all over. There's no entry point. No droppings. No eye sheen. My opinion, no critter circumvented this house and gained entry. It's most likely something loose in the house. Maybe some nail that popped and is now rolling around in the vents."

"But the sound follows me," Sean said. "When I stop, it stops. Have you ever heard of such a thing, or at least an animal doing that?" Sean looked at Ellen. Ellen kept her eyes on the exterminator.

"No. Not when you put it like that, I haven't." The exterminator tipped the bill of his cap as he looked at the ceiling. "If I heard the noise, I'd have a better understanding of what it was. And believe me, if you did have some animal in there, my provoking it would have made it move by now."

All three of them looked at the ceiling. Nothing. Sean hadn't heard the scratching since morning.

"What do you we owe you for the visit?" Ellen asked.

The exterminator smiled. "No charge. Just an evaluation. No harm done." Sean had gotten the exterminator's number from a neighbor. He assumed the neighbor had told the guy what had happened to Danny.

*Try not to overthink it.*

Sean shook the exterminator's hand and told him he'd video-tape the sound and send the clip.

"Not sure that'd help matters." He caught Sean's eyes. "But, I'll take a look at it."

After he left, Ellen began boxing up the house, starting with the nursery. He handed her children's books from the shelves and other knickknacks as she carefully placed them in boxes. With each handoff, Sean eyed the ceiling.

"Is this packing premature? I mean we haven't even gone to that July Fourth party yet. We could hate the people," Sean said.

"Lance told us to stage the house so he can get pictures for the Internet. That's what we're doing. Packing while we do it is like two birds."

"Don't you want to know what happened to the previous owner? Why did he disappear in the middle of the night?"

"Do you think I'm going to tell everyone at the party why we're moving?"

"But we have a reason. Yes, it's personal, but it's not a secret. So, there must be a story behind this Howard guy leaving. You aren't curious?"

*Try not to overthink it.*

"Feel free to drive yourself crazy and—ooh!" Ellen grabbed Sean's hand and placed it on her stomach. He smiled. The baby was still alive.

The second pregnancy didn't allow them a chance to grieve, or reflect, or act irrationally, or fall apart so they could learn as they put themselves back together. Ellen made him attend all the baby classes again. "Maybe we missed something," she said. "Maybe we'll catch it this time." Her denial made him angry, but he had no place to put his anger. He needed to be positive, for the baby, for his marriage. He drank more than usual to combat anger and cynicism. Drinking didn't make him forget; it made him dwell, which he liked. Sometimes he'd tell Ellen he was going to visit his brother, but instead, he'd go to a bar and sit alone and drink.

"He's moving a lot today," Ellen said.

"Now you think it's a 'he,' do you?"

She shrugged and went back to boxing up the room. He stared at the blank wall. *What used to be there?* He looked at Ellen. *Would we have divorced if you weren't pregnant when Danny died? Would we have blamed one another? Would that have pushed you away? Me away?*

*To try not to overthink it.*

He stared at the ceiling, praying the scratch would come back, and then it did. It seemed to fall in rhythm with Ellen's packing. But Ellen never looked up.

@

American flags had been spiked into each yard, yet the flag-pole in the Havenshaw house remained naked. Sean and Ellen were told to park in the Havenshaw garage, to make them feel a part of the street. Lance had left them two baskets on the granite island in the kitchen. One had aged cheeses, a pepperoni stick, and a bottle of red and a bottle of white. The other had bottled water with peanut butter and pretzel rods, which is what Ellen had said was her only pregnancy craving.

"None of this seems strange to you," Sean said, peering out the front window. Several grills were being rolled to the ends of driveways. "It's like we are being courted. Do you think it's because we're—"

"Nope. Don't you dare finish that phrase. The moment you make it about that, you can't make it about anything else." Ellen said.

Ellen kept her stare firm.

*Try not to overthink it.*

The doorbell rang. It was Lance. He looked like he'd walked out of a catalog in his white polo shirt and salmon shorts and Sperry shoes. His arm draped around the waist of a pretty redhead who was at least a decade younger than him.

"Good afternoon, Thatchers," Lance said. Sean shook his hand and told him thanks for the baskets. "How was it pulling into the driveway? Did it feel like home?"

"It did. It really did." Ellen said. "And who is this?"

"This is my beautiful fiancée, Doctor Audrey Pittmann. I introduce her by her first and last name to remind me she isn't taking my last name when we get married this fall." Sean was expecting a smart-ass remark, but then Lance said, "After residency, she's going to be a plastic surgeon. She actually just spent a few months in Africa helping children with cleft palates. If anything, I should take her name." He kissed her cheek. Audrey kissed him back and waved a friendly hello. A grape-sized diamond flashed in the sun.

"That is the biggest diamond I've ever seen," Ellen said. "I'm sorry. I know that's in poor taste to say, but my parents run a jewelry store, and I've never seen anything like that!"

"Really," Audrey said. "Is it around here?"

"In Clintonville. Lee Jewelers."

"I've driven by it, sure," Audrey said.

"It wasn't her first ring." Lance winked. "We had a little issue with the first one, and let's just say, for once, the insurance company didn't win." He laughed and then extended Audrey's hand to showcase the rock. Sean grimaced as Ellen fawned over it, saying something in Chinese and then translating it, saying it is something her father would have said.

Audrey laughed and touched Ellen's shoulder.

*Try not to overthink it.*

Lance clapped. "Off to set-up the Cajun grilling camp. I just wanted to welcome you. Take your time. Look around the house again. We'll see you outside." Lance winked, Audrey waved goodbye, and they headed down the front walk.

Ellen walked back to the kitchen. Sean followed her. "That was some ring," she said. "Lance must sell those big houses along the Scioto."

"Or he's a criminal."

She held up a bottle of wine. "I think I might sneak a glass tonight."

"Seriously, Lance couldn't afford that ring. It had to be twenty thousand dollars."

"Sean, not tonight," she said. "He said something about insurance. Just leave it. Please."

*Try not to overthink it.*

"Oh my!" She grabbed Sean's hand and placed it on the left side of her stomach. "She's feisty today. Maybe she's excited about her new home."

Sean wanted to tell her they should leave and go home. To listen for the scratch. To unpack the boxes. To actually talk about Danny. So when the baby was born they wouldn't forget Danny had been their baby once too.

"Whoo. It's hot."

Lance had set up fans, but they didn't eliminate the July heat.

"I'm spent. Just need to lay down for a bit before we meet everyone."

Ellen used her purse as a pillow. Sean drank his first beer quickly. The second beer went down just as easily. As he opened his third beer he thought about the importance of the summer. No more lesson plans. No more documenting what he does on a daily basis to justify to the state that he actually teaches. No more students grubbing for points. No more begging students to turn in something so they'd pass. This was always a happy time. Reading for pleasure. Sleeping in. Cocktails mid-afternoon. But, it also meant no more distractions, no more reasons to leave the house to make copies or to rewrite a test or to just sit in his classroom and stare at the clichéd posters explaining what teamwork and perseverance were. He sipped his third beer and watched Ellen nap.

@

By the time they reached the end of the driveway, Sean was done with his fourth beer and welcomed the buzz that came with it. "I feel like we live on the set of a television show, Sean. This is so nice. Isn't this so nice?" Ellen waved to a woman across the street. She waved back. Sean thought the woman's wave was aggressive.

"I think she's the pregnant one. I'm going to go say hi."

And just like that, Sean was on his own.

"Hello, future neighbor," a woman said. Sean turned to see a tall, slender blonde in a blue skirt, white tank top, and red heels.

"Hello." Sean pointed at her. "You look like the flag."

"That's the idea." She laughed. Her hair was short, almost buzzed. He couldn't help but stare at her face, trying to figure it out. "Colleen Kellerman." Sean shook her hand and said his name. "Nice to meet you, Sean. I live next door." She walked to him. "I apologize in advance. Old Havenshaw really messed up the unity of the street with the Hardie Plank, and then Lance followed suit and made his all brick." She exhaled. "Maybe they are right to do so. After all, stucco just looks so sad after it rains."

"Unity? Should all houses look the same?"

She shrugged. "You know, I really don't care anymore." She took in a breath and closed her eyes. Even though her face lost expression, Sean couldn't help but assume her eyes were still dancing. She seemed simultaneously likable and unlikable, and the more he felt compelled to judge her, the more he wanted to be her friend. There was something hidden in her face, a sadness, which was an emotion Sean could now see in people as if he had a superpower.

"My son will be a senior in high school next year," she said after Sean asked if she had kids. "Got a 33 on his ACTs. He wants to be a writer."

"I teach high school English," Sean said, pleased with his ability to make small talk. "I once fancied myself as a writer, but I realized I'm much better at helping those that have actual talent." Sean grinned dumbly, still lamenting all those rejection letters for his literary novel using fires to examine gentrification. Ellen had loved his novel. Every word. She even said his saturation of metaphor was what made it so brilliant. How each sentence mattered and if he'd deleted just one phrase, the book would have lost its meaning. It was like a 300-page poem. Thinking of Ellen's support made him wave to her. She was talking to the pregnant woman. The man next to her moved his hand in small circles on the woman's ass.

"An English teacher. Isn't this just serendipitous," the woman said. "Maybe my son could show you some of his work. He's obsessed with the transcendentalists. Everything he writes now sounds so self-important. But don't tell him I said that. He doesn't know I read his stuff. I take pictures of his little notebook he's always writing in when he's not looking. A mother's love."

"The transcendentalists, huh. He wants to 'suck the marrow out of life,' does he?"

"Don't we all." She looked past Sean towards the middle of the cul-de-sac where people started to gather around Lance's grill. Lance kissed his fiancé. "Enjoy the party." Her heels tapped the sidewalk as she headed to her front door and disappeared.

*Was she the saddest woman I've ever met?*

*Try not to overthink it.*

A squirrel jumped in the tree above him, rustling maple leaves. Sean finished his beer. He never considered himself a big drinker, but he supposed over the last six months he'd become one. He'd go ahead and order an extra few at dinner knowing Ellen would drive him home. Then, after she went to sleep, he'd have a few more. Sometimes he'd wake up thinking of Jameson mixed with ginger ale. Although he'd never had a drink in the morning, he was beginning to understand why people did.

Ellen walked over, a half-eaten plate of food in her hand. "Could you," she said, handing him the plate. "I need to use the bathroom. She's punching my bladder."

"Ellen," Sean said, stopping her. "I think the woman who lives next door is sadder than we are."

Above them, a squirrel clawed at something.

"Don't you do that!"

"What?"

"Making this into some sort of novel or something. Like everything means something. These are just people. Same as you and me." She stared at him until he looked her way. "Just enjoy the weather and the fact you don't have to pee every ten minutes, okay?"

The squirrel stopped.

Sean apologized and asked Ellen if she'd bring him a beer. She stared at him, probably trying to gauge how many he'd already had, but instead of asking him, she said, "Social drinking means socializing."

As Ellen hurried away, Sean walked towards Lance Reynolds' house. Ellen would come outside and see him mingling.

*Would that make her happy?*

*Try not to overthink it.*

"Hey, you," an older woman called out. "Yeah, you," she said as Sean pointed at himself. "Come here, would ya?" She was sitting in the mulch bed in front of her porch. She had on a large, red sun hat and her hands were black from the mulch. "Could you hand me that drink? I'm too old anymore to get up and down. I'd rather just stay where I am."

Sean grabbed the blue drink. He could smell the alcohol from the glass, vodka mixed with blue curacao—all alcohol. She took a big gulp.

"Easier to drink after the ice melts." She looked him over. "I don't know you."

"Sean Thatcher. My wife and I are looking at the Havenshaw place."

"A face to the name." She took another gulp. "No secrets on this street. Consider this conversation now part of the public domain." She took another gulp. "Blue drinks are fun. Life should be like my blue drink." She winked. "Free of mixers." She laughed at her own joke, set the drink down, and put her hands back in the mulch.

Sean sensed this woman was sad too, but it was a different sadness than the American flag woman. She seemed to use it as an ally.

"If you don't mind me asking, why are you doing yard work in the middle of the party?" Sean said. Underneath the porch was a nest of cigarette butts. She tossed some mulch to cover them up.

"Which lie do you want?" she said.

"What do you mean?"

She laughed and dug into the mulch with her hands. Ellen walked towards him with a beer. The woman continued to spread mulch.

"I see you're making friends," Ellen said, handing Sean the beer. Sean took an immediate sip. "Hi, I'm Ellen Thatcher." Ellen took back her plate from Sean and ate a watermelon ball.

"Great. All we need is another looker on this street." She looked them over. "You both bi-racial?"

Ellen grabbed Sean's hand and nodded for both of them.

"Bi-racial people are the most beautiful people in the world." The woman sipped her drink. "Something about that unity defines splendor." She grinned. "I used to be all right looking until gravity invaded." She laughed as her hands scraped the surface, revealing a hole in her house.

"Oh my, what happened?" Ellen said, pointing.

"Damn vermin worked its way into my basement. Raccoon the size of Rottweiler. Kept hearing something at night, but ignored it. However, my dog didn't. Thank goodness for Samson." The moment she said his name, a German Shepherd-mix came running from the back yard and nestled next to the woman. "My husband usually dealt with those matters. Now it's all up to me and Samson. That raccoon won the first few rounds, but last I saw of it, the critter was hissing in a cage, off to be incinerated, so I guess I won the war." She cupped her breasts, leaving handprints. "I'd rather have beaten gravity." She smiled. "Now, I'm just digging like a fool, trying to figure how it got in there." She pointed in the dirt. "And I'm pretty sure I just found it."

Sean peered in the hole. A cavern burrowed towards the house.

The lady gulped her drink. "Funny thing curiosity. In its finality the reward is fleeting, but when unsolved, we go mad." She finished the drink and held the glass out for Sean. "Mind doing me a neighborly thing and run inside and make me a new one. The contents are on the island in the kitchen. Fill it with ice and then go half and half. I thank you."

Sean took the glass. The woman stretched her hands behind her and leaned back, enjoying the sun. She started giggling. "If my husband were still alive, he'd probably have eaten the damn thing. Once tried Antelope at a restaurant in Charleston. I asked how it was and his response was 'edible.' Then he kept on eating." She kept on laughing prompting Ellen to join.

Inside, unopened Amazon packages filled the foyer. He made his way to the kitchen and filled the glass with ice, then poured Tito's and Blue Curaçao and mixed it with a spoon. He took a gulp and replaced what he'd drunk. He stopped at the refrigerator. There was a lone postcard from Utah. It was of Angels Landing in Zion National Park. "You were right. I should have stayed. I'll visit soon. David" was written on the back.

*Who's David?*
*Why was he wrong?*
*Try not to overthink it.*

@

The drop in temperature felt nice as night approached. Too many beers in a hot sun had left Sean drunk. Ellen spent a lot of her day with the pregnant woman. Sean kept his distance, afraid he'd mention Danny. He found a man who hated small talk as much as he did, the pregnant woman's husband, so they both stood next to one another drinking in silence. Ellen looked over at them, pleased. She probably thought Sean was making a new best friend. He didn't want her to think differently so he smiled back and then ask the man a question, usually where the closest beer was. Then they'd take turns going to get it. Eventually, Sean asked him about the neighborhood.

"I don't know, you know? I used to hate the suburbs, but now, with the little one on the way . . ." He trailed off. "I mean, it's not too bad."

Lance passed and pointed at the man. "Looking good, Killer. We still on for cards tomorrow?" The man nodded.

*Killer?*
*Friends with Lance?*
*Try not to overthink it.*
Lance pointed at Sean. "We play poker once a month."
"Low stakes," Killer said.

"We actually have a chance at winning since Milton Burnish died." Lance pointed to the house where the woman had been digging in the dirt. "Guy was a shark. Good dude. Made the best brisket."

"My name's Zak by the way."

"Sean."

"Good to meet you, Sean." He handed Sean his beer. "You drink this. I'm exhausted. Just got back in town today. If you want to buy insurance, I'm your guy." He snapped his fingers, then staggered to his home.

Sean yawned. Lance made a joke about Sean's drunkenness and welcomed him to the Peephole. Lance's fiancée had left a few hours back, and since then, he noticed Lance making the rounds. She'd been on call and left for Riverside, the hospital where Danny was born.

*Does that mean something?*

*Try not to overthink it.*

Lance left. He sipped the beer Zak had handed him and looked for Ellen. It was warm, but he didn't care. There was a scratch. He moved to the sound. A girl about seventeen sat under a sycamore tree, carving something in it.

"What'ya doing?"

She looked back. "You buying the house?"

She looked familiar, probably because he'd seen a variation of her year after year at his job. After his failed writing career, he'd asked to stop teaching AP Literature. Surrounded by Faulkner and Ellison and Joyce and Chopin and Kafka and Walker and Baldwin, reminded him of what he didn't become, so he began teaching students who hated high school. Yes, he knew this student. Somehow the rebellious fad never seemed to find its end. Her blonde hair had streaks of green and pink. She wore combat boots and a short black skirt. The band name on her t-shirt was also familiar to Sean. He'd seen it on other t-shirts in the school halls, but he didn't actually know any of their music.

"Thinking about it, yeah," Sean said, smiling. Oddly, talking to a teenager was the most comfortable he'd felt all night.

"Howard Havenshaw was a dick."

*Try not to overthink it.*

"I'm Mr. Thatcher. Or Sean. You can call me Sean."

"Sean. Got any weed?"

"Medicinal or back alley?"

She stared at him like she was trying to figure out if he was cool or just some lame-o trying too hard.

"What's your name?"

She shrugged. "Nikki."

"Have I met your parents tonight?"

"If you met my mom, did you tell her to fuck off?"

"Did not tell anyone to 'fuck off' so, guess I didn't meet your mom." Sean had learned responding with profanity when his students used it took away its power.

"You see that woman over there, standing on the porch?" Nikki said. Sean looked and nodded. The woman had been there all night. No one had talked to her, but now, the woman who'd been digging in the dirt, sat next to her. "She's crazy. Like seriously, clinically crazy. Her son died in Afghanistan this year, but she was crazy long before that." She turned to the tree and continued carving. "Her husband remarried last month. He's a good guy. Really is. But she's all alone now, and that's how we all end."

"Alone?"

She scratched the tree and tossed the rock. "Forgetting what it means to fight."

"Fighting is the only thing we can do."

"Is that why you're moving here? Part of the fight?"

"Actually, yeah."

He pinched his face, hoping not to cry. Nikki stared at him. She stood and took a step forward into the floodlights. "You didn't see any other kids here tonight, did you? Tall, skinny kid?"

Sean shook his head.

Nikki nodded. Tears streamed her cheeks, yet not one muscle in her face changed. "You ever lose someone close to you, and you want to be mad at them and blame them, but deep down you know it's your fault. You know it's your fault, but you don't do anything to make it better, and since you don't do anything to

make it better, everything you do really just makes life worse?"
Her tears made the sadness in her eyes sparkle.

"I have. Yeah."

"I used to have this thing I did online to help, but I don't
have that anymore." She looked down the cul-de-sac. "Here's the
million dollar question: how come knowing other people feel the
same pain as you doesn't eliminate the loneliness? I mean, fuck,
it's like we are all fighting to monopolize misery." She shook her
head. "The world is a mess and no one wants to clean it."

"What do you mean?"

She shrugged. "There's no profit in cleaning up messes." She
pulled a flag up from the ground. "'Merica!"

She walked past him, towards the darkened woods behind
her house. Her phone glowed in the night as she sent a text. Two
houses down Lance took his phone out of his salmon shorts.

*Try not to overthink it.*

Sean moved to the tree and ran his hand over the carving:
FUCK THE PEEPHOLE.

People started saying their goodnights. Sean made his way
towards his wife. He heard Ellen laughing in the darkness two
houses away. A thin, good-looking man was cleaning his grill.
Sean hadn't talked to him yet. The man called Sean over. "Sean
Thatcher, right? Bruce Whiting." They shook hands. There was a
brief pause. Sean thought how nice it would be to live in a place
that had such a loud, calming silence.

"What do you think of our little street?" the man said, spray-
ing his grill with cleaner.

"It's nice."

"It's safe. And if that's what you're looking for, then, look no
further."

For some reason, Sean thought of Danny when he was nine
weeks old and how he'd carefully wiped goop out of Danny's left
eye because of a blocked tear duct. There'd been a storm outside
and the wind moved a tree branch against the bedroom window.
Danny turned to the soft sound of the branch scraping and
smiled. It'd been his first genuine smile.

Bruce finished cleaning the utensils. He eased the grill backward on its wheels. "Heard your wife is expecting. My wife is two months pregnant. We've obeyed that superstition of not telling anyone before three months, but I'm telling you."

This must've been the other couple Lance had spoken about.

"Why?" Sean asked

The man grinned. The whites of his eyes shone in the darkness. "I don't know, but it feels good to say it."

The woman dressed like a flag was gathering all the little flags that lined the yards. Lance Reynolds shouted goodnights from the front porch. "Thatchers! We'll talk business tomorrow. Havenshaw said he'd keep making payments on his house until your house sold. This deal is as good as done. Welcome to the Peephole!"

Everyone joined in. "Welcome to the Peephole!"

Lance flashed his porch light once. Was it a signal?

*Try not to overthink it.*

The good-looking man rolled his grill up the driveway. A pretty woman was waiting for him in the lit garage. They kissed passionately, the way teenagers do when they feel love for the first time.

Ellen hugged the pregnant women she'd befriended and hobbled towards Sean. She held her back and moved like she had ten blisters on each foot. "I'm beat. You need to drive home," she said.

"I can't," he said, gulping down the last bit of his can. He thought she was going to frown or give that disappointed look, the one she'd perfected over the years when he'd done something wrong, but all she did was smile and said she was happy he'd a good time.

They walked towards the Havenshaw place. The woman dressed like a flag stood at the end of her driveway and removed her red heels.

"Hope you two had fun," she said, rubbing her buzzed head.

"Colleen Kellerman, right? Yes. We did. We had so much fun." Ellen said. "Thank you for inviting us."

"Colleen Irving actually. Divorce is official as of yesterday. Please don't give me that look. Best thing that's ever happened to me. Sean, I saw you talking to Nikki. Did you see where she went?"

"Yeah, she went that way," Sean pointed to the darkness behind the houses.

Colleen's headshake slowly turned into a nod. "Thank you." Colleen hugged both of them. "I make the best lasagna. I'll bring it over when you move in. No one wants to cook that day and pizza is so cliché." She paused. "Nikki went to the woods?" She closed her eyes, took a deep breath. When her eyes opened she stared at Lance Reynolds' house and then looked at her bare feet. "Long day." She gave another hard look to the woods before walking up her driveway and disappearing in the darkness of the garage.

Ellen grabbed Sean's hand.

"Sean."

*Try not to overthink it.*

They entered Havenshaw's front door—as if they lived there—and walked to the kitchen. Ellen opened the refrigerator and grabbed the bottle of water that had been in the basket.

"I'm so tired." She nodded as she yawned. "Celia and I saw you getting along with . . ."

"Zak."

"Yes. Zak. Celia and Zak. And they don't want to know what they are having either. A surprise, just like us."

Ellen buried her head in Sean's chest, making a soft, pleasant moan.

"I really can't drive," she said. "This little one has just zapped me. I need a quick nap. Then we'll go." She smiled and went back to the spot where she'd slept earlier. "Come here and keep me warm."

On the way in, Sean had gotten a blanket from the trunk of the car. He spread it out on the floor. He took a bag of hotdog buns and set them down as a pillow for her, and then he inserted a package of hamburger buns between her knees.

"This is nice. Thank you. Just a quick nap," Ellen said. "Just a quick nap and then we can go." She curled the other side of the blanket over her and began her usual soft snore that had become something of a hypnotic calm to Sean over the years, helping him sleep.

His phone, which he had forgotten on the counter, beeped. He ignored it and lay next to Ellen. He looked at the recessed lighting in the great room and wondered how he'd replace the bulbs when they burned out. He spooned Ellen. The berry scent was gone from her hair, replaced with summer. He angled his right arm to support his head as his left draped over her. He cupped the bottom of her pregnant belly. No movement. The baby must be asleep, like her mother. He looked up. One of the bulbs flickered. He closed his eyes and listened.

# About the Author

JOSH PENZONE lives in Ohio with his wife and daughter. He has been nominated for a Pushcart Prize and his fiction has appeared in *Five on the Fifth*, *Eunoia Review*, *Blue Lake Review*, *Junto Magazine* and elsewhere.

www.ingramcontent.com/pod-product-compliance
Lightning Source LLC
Chambersburg PA
CBHW020640250626
47154CB00008B/2750